BILLY

GUARDIAN DEFENDERS

KRIS MICHAELS

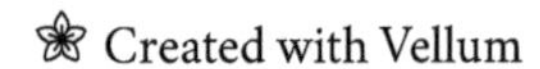
Created with Vellum

CHAPTER 1

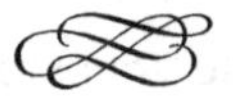

Billy Pearson rode the elevator up to the clinic. He'd heard from Mike White Cloud that a sniper from Russia had been admitted, recovering from tetanus, of all things. He wanted to meet the guy. Simply because he was curious but also, to tell the truth, because he was bored. Winters in South Dakota were when he and Asp built new weapons, trained with the twins, Adam, and Mike, and worked on the course they'd developed for Guardian. Of course, the range was fucking frigid that time of year, so both he and Asp were on call for missions.

He opened the door to the supply closet and exited into the hallway of the small clinic housed aboveground. He made his way to the room Chief said the sniper was in and knocked on the door, then stopped. A tiny blonde woman turned to look at him from the hospital bed.

"Yes?" Her accent was clearly Russian.

"I am so sorry." Billy gave her his best smile. "I was told someone else was staying in this room." A sniper, not a teenager.

"Who were you looking for? I believe I am the only one admitted to the hospital, or that is what my doctor said." The woman cocked her head at him, and that was when Billy noticed her eyes. Big, blue, and hard as ice.

"I was told a Russian sniper was here." Leaning against the door frame, he crossed his arms over his chest.

"This is correct. I am here." The woman winced as she twisted on the bed to look at him. "What is it I can do for you?"

Billy stared at her for a moment, then laughed. "That is freaking awesome." Stepping away from the door frame, he walked into the room and grabbed a plastic chair from alongside the wall. He moved it closer to the bed and sat down, crossing his boot over his knee. "What type of weapon do you use? What caliber of bullet? What's the maximum effective range? How far can you reliably shoot with it? What's the training like? How often do you practice? Is there a cadre of snipers in the Russian military, or are they assigned to units? Who's the best you've ever seen? What was the most impressive shot you've ever taken?" He wanted to know it all. He, Asp, and now Alex had compared notes so often that their memories had almost become his. He was jonesing for new information.

The woman blinked at him. "Who *are* you?"

Well, shit, that might help, Billy. "Oh, damn, sorry." He stood up and extended his hand. "Billy Pearson. I work with Guardian and do the same job as you. So, the interest is legitimate."

The woman reached out and shook his hand. Her grip was strong, and she looked him straight in the eye. "Forgive me, Billy, but I am not going to tell you a thing until I know it is permitted to do so." She withdrew her hand.

"Ah." Billy blinked, not expecting that answer. "Who do I need to get in here to tell you it's okay?" He'd put a jack under any ass on the ranch so he could visit with her.

"Malice," she said and looked at him.

"Huh." Billy frowned for a minute. "Well, okay. I know where to go to get that done. Don't go anywhere, okay?" He grabbed the chair and stepped backward.

"She won't be leaving for the foreseeable future."

An ice-cold shiver ran down Billy's back. *Mandy*? Billy felt his gut drop. He turned slowly and almost passed the fuck out. *What in the hell? Or should he say,* Who *in the hell?*

A brunette with long, thick, wavy hair smiled at him. The same crooked smile, the same fucking voice. And her eyes. Fuck him standing. Those eyes were the only thing different. Amanda had green eyes; this woman had brown, but it didn't matter. She was the spitting image of Amanda. Holy hell, it was as if a ghost from his past had stepped from the shadows into the light.

The woman walked into the room and extended her hand. "Hi. I'm Lillian Montrose, her doctor. She's going to be my guest for a while."

Billy stared at the woman who could be the reincarnation of the woman he'd been … forced to leave behind. The hair was wrong, too long and too dark, but God in heaven, she could be Amanda's twin. His heart pounded against his rib cage. His brain slapped him with a horrific symphony of shock and déjà vu. He was rooted to the spot. He couldn't move, he couldn't speak, and fuck him, he was afraid if he did, the apparition in front of him would disappear. He wasn't sure if he wanted her to fade away, or if he wanted her to never leave.

The doctor frowned and looked from him to the woman in the hospital bed. "Was it something I said?"

"Maybe?" The Russian shrugged.

The doctor turned back to him. "Are you all right?"

Billy snapped his mouth shut. "Yeah. Fine." He cleared his throat. "Excuse me." He pushed against the wall, giving the ghost from his past a wide berth, and slipped into the hallway.

"What in the world did I do to him?" Billy heard the doctor ask as he race-walked to the supply closet and the hidden elevator door. Fuck him sideways and ten ways to Sunday. He got in the elevator and jammed his thumb against the only button five or ten times. The door shut, and he dropped back against the far wall.

"Why? Why now? God, I thought I was past this." He'd buried that life when he buried Sergeant William Mackenzie Robinson. Mac was gone. Forever. He was Billy Pearson now. No one but Alex and his spotter, Nail, knew about his past, and that was unavoidable. He was supposed to be over this.

Billy bolted out of the elevator as soon as the door opened. He went straight to the armory, then checked out his weapon and five boxes of ammo before putting on his fucking bunny suit. He needed lead therapy in the most emergent way possible, and he needed it right the fuck now.

HE WAS on his third box of custom-made shells when he heard Asp behind him. "How much do you want to bet it has something to do with an upcoming mission?"

"Dude, even if he spent a thousand rounds, it wouldn't make him a better shot. He's reached his apex." Alex drawled in reply.

"Fuck you both," Billy said, sending another bullet through the hole he'd blown in his target. He then ejected the round and loaded another.

"Nah, not my type," Alex said after the percussion of the bullet firing ceased. "He's more your type."

Billy assumed he was talking to Asp. "No, not

really. I prefer mine more female and a hell of a lot sexier than that."

"Fuck you both," Billy said again, but a small smile tipped his lips up. He fired again, ejecting the round, and laid his weapon down. Only then did he roll onto his back and glare up at the two men behind him. "Why are you here?"

"Well, let's see …" Asp rubbed his chin. "It's below zero. We had a curriculum meeting a half hour ago, and one-third of the teaching staff is out here wasting ammo. That about covers it, right?" Asp looked over at Alex.

"Yeah, oh, and that one-third of the teaching staff was the one who called the meeting, so neither one of us knew what in the hell we were talking about."

"That's about usual." Billy rolled his eyes and sat up.

Asp held out a hand. "What the fuck has you riled up?"

Billy gripped his friend's glove and pulled himself up. "Ever seen a ghost?"

Alex snorted. "Yeah, when I saw you after you died."

Asp pointed at Alex. "What he said."

Billy closed his eyes. "Smart asses everywhere."

"Takes one to know one," Alex said with a laugh.

"Yeah, what he said," Asp repeated.

Billy opened his eyes and pinned Asp with a dead-on, laser-focused stare. "I'm being serious."

Asp's demeanor changed immediately. "What's up?"

Billy looked at Alex. "Can I talk with Asp in private? We'll do the meeting another time."

Alex nodded. "If you need anything, I've got your back."

"I know," Billy said. "But this goes back to our time in the agency together. I'll explain later when I get my head around what's happening." He extended his hand, which Alex grabbed.

"Whatever it takes," Alex said before heading back toward the compound.

"As long as it takes," both he and Asp said in unison as they watched their friend walk away.

"What's happening, my man?" Asp bent over and picked up the two brass casings he hadn't policed.

"I saw Amanda today."

"Ms. Marshall? Why is that a problem?" Asp dropped the casings into the catch bucket and stood up.

"No, my Amanda. Mandy. Or at least I thought I did." Billy sighed and crossed his arms over his chest. "But it wasn't her. Mac, it was a mind fuck." He rubbed his face with his glove.

"Dude, you haven't called me Mac since Colombia. Come on, grab that ammo, and let's get inside where it's warm, and you can explain this shit to me."

Asp grabbed his gun, and Billy understood why. He was talking like a fucking lunatic. "I'm not insane." Billy grabbed the ammo and the brass bucket and headed toward the compound.

"Never said you were." Asp fell into step with him.

"You thought it." Billy sighed.

"Maybe." Asp chuckled. "But I've always thought you were a bubble off-center."

"I went to the hospital today to see the sniper," Billy said as they trudged over the frozen ground.

"What?" Asp frowned and looked at him. "What in the hell are you talking about?"

"Mike told me a Russian sniper was staying at the hospital. So, me being me, I went to talk to her. I wanted to know all the goods, get me?"

"Her?" Asp stopped and shook his head. "A female?"

"Yeah, she was in a hospital bed. She was a small blonde, about five foot nothing, and maybe ninety or a hundred pounds. A tiny little thing who looks maybe eighteen years old."

"And she reminded you of Mandy?" Asp narrowed his eyes at him.

"No." Billy huffed out a breath of air and watched the cloud of his breath float away. "She told me she wouldn't talk to me unless some dude named Malice said it was okay. I don't know who that is, but I figured Mike would, right? So, I was putting the chair back by the wall, and I heard that voice. *Mandy's* voice."

Asp's eyebrows rose. "As a ghost?"

Billy rolled his eyes and started walking again. "Just forget it."

"No, dude, you got to help me understand this," Asp said as he fell into step with him again.

"The sniper's doctor." Billy stopped again and looked at his friend. "Mac, she's a dead ringer for Mandy. The hair is a bit different, darker, and longer, and the eye color is off, but her face, voice, her smile, her body. Fuck, it's like someone cloned Mandy and dropped her here."

"What doctor is this?" Asp's confusion was plastered across his face.

"She said her name was Lillian Montrose." Billy turned and started walking again. "It's fucking eerie." Billy opened the door in one of the sheds and waited for Asp to come in. He hit the button under the bottom shelf, and the fake wall moved, opening the elevator door.

Once they'd entered, Asp hit the button to close the door. "She's probably not that close. You could be over-exaggerating."

Billy shook his head. He knew what and who he'd seen. "No. I'm not." He'd watched from afar as Mandy struggled for years after his CIA-created death. The sons of bitches had fucked both him and Asp. Mandy had finally met a guy about five years ago, and that one didn't abuse her. *She* was happy, and the two of them had started a family. A little boy. But it had been two … maybe three years since he'd checked on her or thought about her. Until today.

"So, let's go talk to this ghost," Asp said casually as they walked back to the armory. "After you clean this rifle."

Billy dropped the brass bucket and put the unspent ammo back on the shelf. He logged in the amount he used and initialed the inventory sheet. Asp didn't get it. The resemblance was uncanny, and … Well, hell, it felt like someone had ripped open his chest and put a big fucking fist around his heart and squeezed. Billy rolled his eyes at himself as he put the clipboard back on the nail it hung from. He was such a sap and, today, a chicken shit. "No way, my man. I'm not mentally ready for that. Not freaking the fuck out twice in one day." He poured the brass into the recycling barrel.

Asp started disassembling the rifle as he pulled down the cleaning rods, patches, attachments, and lubricating oil. Billy took the upper receiver, while Asp assembled a rod to clean the barrel. They were quiet as they worked. "This doc really looks like Mandy?"

Billy nodded. "Sounds like her, too." That bedroom velvet type of voice that was just husky enough to be sexy as fuck. "That's what first hit me, man. My gut dropped to the floor."

"Does Mandy have any sisters?" Asp finished boring the barrel and switched attachments to run a patch through the thing.

"No. She's an only child." Billy used a brush on the firing pin of his weapon to get all the residue off. "I wasn't expecting it. Man, she knocked me for a loop. I tucked tail and got the hell out of the clinic."

"Well, when you're ready, we'll go over together." Asp pulled the dirty patches out of the barrel and switched them out for clean ones.

"I don't need you to play babysitter." And he sure as hell wouldn't return to the clinic anytime soon.

"I'm curious now. Besides, didn't you want to talk to that sniper?" Asp held up the barrel and looked through it. Obviously not satisfied, he put another patch through the rod and shoved it back down the barrel.

He did want to talk to her. "I'm not sure how that woman carried a weapon this size." He chuckled. "She was a bitty thing."

"Never judge a book by its cover," Asp said as he peered down the barrel again before grunting and grabbing a rag to wipe off the outside of it. "Look at Joy. A little wisp of nothing and deadlier than any of us."

Billy nodded as he reassembled the upper receiver before turning his attention to wiping it down. "True. What or who is a Malice?" Billy looked at Asp.

The man paused and focused on him. "Why?"

"That's who the sniper said could clear her to

talk." Billy put the rag down and took the barrel from Asp to reassemble his weapon.

"Never met him. Is he on the property?"

Billy looked up at Asp. "Not the question I asked."

Asp crossed his arms over his chest. "He's like me."

"What?" Billy snorted out a laugh. "There's nobody quite like you ..." Billy's gaze shot over to Asp. "Oh."

Asp's eyebrow lifted, and his head cocked. "I'll see if I can make contact and get you permission to talk to her."

"That would be mighty decent of you." He didn't want an assassin pissed off at him. He had the opportunity to go the route Asp had followed when he joined Guardian, but he'd had enough of that working for the agency or for Stratus, as it turned out. Now, he taught and went out on missions when teams needed an overwatch. It suited where he was in his life and more than paid the bills. Hell, he didn't have many expenses, and the money he was pulling down was ten times better than he'd ever earned.

"That's me, a decent guy. Are you coming over

tonight for dinner? Lyric is making a pork roast with all the fixings."

Billy snapped his gaze up to look at his friend. "Is she?"

"Yep." Asp smiled widely. "She's baking bread, too."

"Man, I thought you were insane for building a house that was mostly kitchen, but damn … Yeah, if you don't mind, I'll be there."

"That kitchen is her pride and joy. If she's happy, I'm happy." Asp walked over to the sink to wash his hands.

"Speaking of which, how are the fertility treatments going?" Asp and Lyric had been trying for a family for years and were now on the second round of treatments. From what Asp said, the medical aspect of the process was damn hard on Lyric.

"We're hoping for the best. If this doesn't work, we're going to look into adoption." Asp pulled two paper towels out of the dispenser and wiped his hands. "She was so disappointed last time; it fucking gutted me." Asp looked over at him. "I'm sorry about what happened to you today. Shit like that … I know what happened to Mandy. The agency screwed her. But she's happy now. What about you? When are you going to move on with your life?"

Billy chuckled. "I'm not a hermit."

"But you aren't dating."

Billy lifted his hands and turned around. "What single women do you see out here?"

"What about Allison?" Asp asked as he crossed his arms and leaned against the wall.

"Yeah, she's nice, but, man, she's a hard nut. I thought maybe, but there's no way I'm going to work that hard to date someone. Get me?" Allison had caught his interest once upon a time, but she was a hard woman to get to know. He'd dropped it after a couple of tries.

"Do you want me to look into the doctor's background? It wouldn't be hard to pull in a favor or two."

"Nah. That's not necessary." Billy wiped off his assembled weapon and put it back in the rack where it belonged. "I think I shot the shock out of my system." *Maybe.*

"All right. I'll find Malice and sort out talking to the sniper. Did you get her name?"

Billy blinked and paused as he reached for the soap at the sink. "Dude, no, I didn't."

Asp walked up beside him. "See you at six?"

"I'll be there." Billy dried his hands as he listened to Asp's retreating steps. He stared down at the crumpled brown paper in his hands. The shock *had* dissipated. What remained now was a healthy dose of ... caution. He couldn't let the woman's likeness to Mandy affect him, and he knew it would. He'd give her a wide birth. Hell, he was as healthy as a horse. He never went to the clinic. He shot the paper through the air and swooshed a three-pointer from across the room. "And the crowd goes wild!" Billy lifted his hands in the air and spun toward the door. Life was good. Damn good.

CHAPTER 2

Lillian Montrose sat down behind the desk she'd been given by Adam Cassidy, the full-time doctor at Guardian's annex. Leaning back in the chair, she stared out the window. The handsome man she'd chased out of Anya's room that morning was still on her mind. What in the hell had she done to make him act like she had the plague? Anya had said the man was chatty and happy until she walked in.

She shook her head. Reactions like that were caused by something. Her cell phone rang in her pocket. She pulled it out of her white coat and smiled at the name as she accepted the call. "Abe! Shouldn't you be getting ready for your bachelor's party?"

"I'm on Pacific time, lady. I have a couple of hours. Are you sure I can't get you out here for the wedding?" Abe was her partner on Mercy Team Five. He was her physician's assistant and the best lab tech she'd ever worked with. Moving to Guardian from their last employment had been a drastic transfer, but after ... Well, Abe and his brother had thrown her a lifeline, and she took it. They'd worked together for the last four years, and Lillian couldn't ask for a better teammate.

"No way I can. My patient is doing better, but with Adam out of pocket, I'm the only doctor here." Lillian hated missing his wedding, but with the tension between Abe's fiancée and her, it was better she wasn't at the ceremony.

"Are you sure it isn't because of Heather?" Abe's serious tone rumbled across the line.

"It's her day, Abe. I know she doesn't really care for me. It's better this way."

Abe sighed, "She's jealous."

Lillian closed her eyes. "I've never given her a reason to feel that way." Abe was a brother to her.

"I know. It's irrational, and I've told her that, but ... I love her, Lil. She's worth the effort."

"Which is why you're going to make such a wonderful husband and daddy."

"Whoa the horses there, cowgirl. Let me get married before you pin the dad title on my collar."

"I guess I could do that." Lillian laughed.

"Now, we just need to get you a decent man." Abe chuckled.

"Right. I can't see that happening anytime soon, especially not with how I scare men away."

"What?" Abe sounded confused.

"Okay, promise you won't laugh?"

"Nope. Not in the slightest." Abe chuckled, making her smile.

"Fine. Well, this morning, I went into my patient's room and overheard a gentleman who was visiting her. I made a comment, nothing abrasive or dismissive, you know, just jumping into the conversation, and the guy turned around like I'd busted him over the head with a beer bottle. Real slow, you know. Like one of those moments in the movies. The big bad guy gets pissed off and turns around in slow-motion with daggers in his eyes."

"Okay, you set the stage. Now, reel me in. What happened?"

"Well, nothing. I introduced myself and held out my hand." Lillian shook her head. "Abe, it was like I had a fire-breathing dragon head and was as ugly as Methuselah. He backed into the wall, scraped along it, and rolled out the door, trying to avoid me."

"Bullshit," Abe scoffed.

"I wish," Lillian responded. "I have no idea what I did."

"No, no, no," Abe said in a hurry. "This isn't on you. This guy is the one with the problem. Don't go there."

Lillian smiled. "Thanks."

"Seriously, Lil, this guy is a jerk. You're a wonderful person, and it's taken years for you to overcome that bastard. None of that was your fault, no matter what he said. You know it; your therapist and I know it."

"Yeah, still, sometimes stuff like this just kind of hits me hard, you know?"

"I get it, but listen, that situation and this one are two totally different things. Dion was a narcissist, and he used you, isolated you, and then dumped you. The man shouldn't be allowed to practice medicine. I can't believe he found a job in Europe." The bitterness in Abe's voice was one of the reasons she adored him. He always had her six, like she had his.

"I know. Still, whenever something like this happens, I guess I get flashbacks." Dion was the king of gaslighting, and for several years, Lillian had wondered if she were slowly going insane.

"Yeah, that's understandable, but don't go there with this guy, okay? If he has an issue, that's on him. You're one of the best people on the face of the Earth."

"Tell that to Heather, huh?" Lillian deflected.

"She knows. That's why she's jealous." Abe chuckled. "But we had a long heart-to-heart last night after her parents and mine went to their hotels. I love her, and she loves me. The work we do for Guardian has nothing to do with that. She admitted she knew there was no reason to be jealous, but get this, you're too pretty to be a doctor."

Lillian snorted in surprise. "I'm too pretty? My God, Heather is the most beautiful woman I've ever seen."

"Which is what I told her. You can't hold a candle to her."

Lillian frowned. "Hey!"

Abe laughed. "In my eyes, Lil. I've only got eyes for her."

"Oh, okay." Lillian smiled and stared out the window. The snow had started to come down again. "Don't do anything stupid tonight. Your bride would never forgive you."

"Nah, I gave Cash his instructions. No strippers. I think we're going to drink, smoke cigars, and play poker."

"And you trust your brother to follow the rules?" Lillian's eyebrows raised to her hairline. Cash was a crazy man when he wasn't working as the team leader of Foxtrot Team for Guardian.

"Well, *now* I don't. Thanks for making that awkward," Abe chided.

She laughed. "Text me after you get hitched. No, wait. Don't do that. Don't call or text, and wipe this call off your call log. Pay one hundred percent attention to your bride. I will talk to you when you're back from your honeymoon and I'm through with my time here at the annex."

"That's four months, Lil." Abe sounded incredulous.

"Yep. I love you like a brother, Abe, and I want you and Heather to be happy. That means she doesn't worry about me; you give her your undivided attention. Work will be here when you get back."

"Evie is taking care of your house, right?"

Lillian smiled. "Yep. She's staying there. It's closer to the college than her sister's apartment." Evie had been a lab tech, but she was now enrolled in a nursing program at Washington State University in Spokane. Lillian and Abe knew her from their time at Plume Laboratories.

"And all your bills are on autopay?"

"Yes, Dad." Lillian laughed.

"All right, all right, I'll back off."

"That'll be the day," Lillian shot back at him.

"You're right. I'll let you go now, but if you need anything, call me. We're *partners*." Abe stressed the last word.

"And I've got your back," Lillian reminded him. "That's why you're going to hang up now and go get your drunk on."

Abe sighed. "Thank you for being an awesome friend."

"Don't get all mushy on me, Costello." Lillian's eyes filled with tears. "I'll see you in a couple of months."

"Take care of you, Lil."

"I will if you will."

"Deal," Abe said. "Bye."

"Bye." She disconnected and placed her phone on the desk. She jumped up and spun at the sound of a throat clearing behind her. "Holy hell, Mal! Why would you do that? I could have died." Lillian grabbed her chest.

Malice's face split into a wide smile. "And yet, you didn't."

"No thanks to you." She tossed a pen at him. He caught it and tossed it back to her. She wasn't as graceful catching the thing, but after bobbling it a couple of times, she snagged it.

"How's Anya today?"

Lillian frowned. "Haven't you been to see her yet?"

"I have, but I want a medical opinion." Malice leaned against the door.

"She's on the mend. The infection came roaring back as soon as the meds were stopped, which was what I expected. I want her in the clinic until we're sure it's gone. We're going to make sure that infection is beaten this time."

"I appreciate that," Malice said. "Any restrictions on diet? There's some candy she really likes. I'd thought I'd go to town and pick it up."

"Candy is fine as long as she's eating the rest of her meals. I might suggest card games, board games, and such. Perhaps coloring books."

Malice's head whipped in her direction. "Excuse me?"

"Coloring books? They have them for adults now. Colored pencils and such. It's calming and takes up time. She's going to get bored when you're not here."

"Is there any restriction about me being here, like visiting hours and such?" Mal's forehead formed furrows over his eyes.

"What? No. Just no overnight guests. She needs the sleep, and so do you." Lillian had seen the connection between the two, and she was a little envious of how deeply they cared for each other. But that niggle of envy passed without much thought. The rightness of them was pretty amazing.

Malice nodded and stepped away from the door frame. "She said someone came to visit earlier. Do you know who that was?"

"No, but then again, I arrived at the annex the same time you did, so I don't know many people."

Malice nodded casually. "Okay, just wondering. Thanks, Lillian. Do you need anything from town? I'm going to make a run for that candy."

"No, thank you. The quarters they gave me have everything I'll ever need."

"This complex is pretty amazing," Malice agreed. "I'll be back in a couple hours."

"I'll have handed things off to the night staff by then. I'll see you tomorrow?"

"You can bet on that." He gave her a two-finger salute, then turned to leave.

Lillian sat back at her desk and pulled the laptop over. She only had to complete notes on one patient, which wouldn't take long. After a weird day, she was looking forward to a hot bubble bath, a glass of wine, and an old movie from the Blu-ray library downstairs. With four months of almost no work to look forward to, time to do some self-care and relax in the middle of South Dakota sounded perfect. Like the vacation she needed but didn't want to take. She always preferred to keep busy, and her new assignment was the perfect combination of work and rest.

CHAPTER 3

Billy laughed at the three kittens zooming through the kitchen into the front room of Asp and Lyric's home. "They *are* batshit crazy." He popped a roasted baby carrot into his mouth.

"That they are. There's never a dull moment with those three. I'll be so happy when Doc Macy finds homes for them. Fostering these lunatics keeps me on my toes, but be careful. They've been known to jump on the counters. The tiger-striped one scared me to death, and I almost lost the pork roast I was pulling out of the oven," Lyric said as she stirred the gravy. "Isaac, would you feed them?"

"On it." He reached down and grabbed the

orange one as it tried to zoom past him. The other two followed him to the laundry room, where their food bowls were located.

Billy chuckled at the assassin doing household chores and being a great husband. It was the best thing to come out of that mission in Colombia. "Thanks for the invite. When are you going to get tired of me eating you out of house and home?" Billy picked up another carrot.

"You're welcome anytime, and if I make enough to feed Isaac, I'm making enough to feed an army."

"I heard that!" Isaac roared from the laundry room.

"I don't care!" Lyric yelled back to him. Laughing, she took the pan off the burner and poured the dark brown gravy into a bowl. "Take this to the table, would you?" She motioned to the gravy.

"You got it. Veggies, too?"

"Is there any left?" Lyric laughed the question.

"Ha, as you said, enough for an army." Billy placed that and the platter of roasted veggies onto the table.

Lyric pushed her hair back and pointed to the butcher block holding her knives. "Could you do me a favor and slice the roast? I need to take a quick break."

"You got it." Billy practically lived at Asp and Lyric's. Even though his and Lyric's introduction had been rough, they'd become good friends. He enjoyed spending time with the couple but made sure his visits were limited to give them time alone. He didn't want to be *that* person.

"Where's my woman?" Asp asked as he came back into the kitchen.

"Taking a quick break," Billy said, grabbing a knife from the butcher block.

"You got this? I'm going to go wash up."

"I can handle slicing the roast, but don't take too long. There might not be any left when you get back."

Asp growled a line of cuss words, and Billy barked out a laugh that followed Asp out of the kitchen.

He stuck the carving fork into the top of the roast and started slicing. Lyric was a hell of a chef, and her equipment, including knives, was the best. The knife moved through the roast, cutting perfect slices. The kittens ran out of the laundry room, and he chuckled at the sounds of them doing zoomies on the hardwood floor. He caught their craziness out of the corner of his eye as he sliced through the roast. The smell was out of the world.

Billy lifted the knife for another slice, and that was when shit went bonkers.

The feel of needles being implanted in his calf and then up the back of his leg jerked him upright. The kitten climbing his leg made it to his back, and Billy hissed, dropping his hold on the butcher knife. It clattered to the counter.

The tiger-striped kitten launched onto the counter and landed on the handle of the butcher knife. Billy reached for the cat with one hand and the knife with the other as it flew up and into the air. The other kitten clawed its way to his shoulder as he grabbed the falling knife.

"Oh, shit!" Lyric yelled and grabbed at the furball. Only the kitten's claws were buried in his shoulder. But that bit of hell didn't bother him too much. He stood with his hand cupped and the knife's blade inserted into his palm, blood dripping from his fisted grip.

"Oh no!" Lyric gasped when she saw the blood. "Isaac!"

Asp ran into the kitchen. "What in the hell?" Billy hunched over the counter, holding the knife so it didn't wobble as Lyric tried to extract the kitten's needles of death, one paw at a time, but every time one paw came out, another attached.

"How the hell did you do that?" Asp asked as he grabbed a clean kitchen towel.

Billy hissed as Lyric continued to try to pry the kitten off his back. "Oh, you know, I had nothing better to do than become a jungle gym for these little assholes."

Asp grunted. "Come over here."

Billy moved to the sink. He hadn't ungripped the blade because he was pretty sure the droplets of blood would turn into a spatter. He'd sliced himself pretty good.

Asp ducked down and looked at where his hand clasped the edge of the blade. Lyric finally got the cat's claws out of his shoulder and grabbed the one he was still holding in his other hand by the scruff of the neck.

Asp stood up and grimaced. "Dude, that doesn't look good."

"Yeah, I figured." It seemed like it was his day for all the fun, didn't it?

"You're going to need stitches," Lyric said from beside him as she held the murder kittens to her chest.

Asp nodded. "She's right. Go ahead and relax your fist."

Lyric put her hand on Billy's other arm. "No, don't do that. What if he bleeds out?"

"From a hand wound?" Asp asked.

"From a cut?" Billy said at the same time. "I didn't hit an artery."

Lyric looked from one to the other. "Well, fine, but if he dies, it's on you."

Billy blinked, then looked from Lyric to Asp. Both he and Asp started laughing at the same time. "Don't die on me," Asp said.

"Wouldn't dream of it," he said, opening his hand. He winced as he examined the slice across the palm of his hand. It wouldn't kill him, but it would be a pain in the ass while it healed. Asp wrapped the dishtowel around his hand. "Well, hell, looks like I'm going to visit Doc Cassidy."

"Hold on, I'll grab our coats."

"You don't need to go with me. Stay and eat your dinner."

Asp looked at the roast and then at him. "I like cold roast, too. Babe, I'll be back as soon as I get Billy tucked in."

"Dude, I can walk to the clinic myself," Billy said to Asp's back.

"I'll keep dinner warm for both of you," Lyric

said as Asp went for the coats. "I'm so sorry. I've never seen a cat climb a person before."

Billy smiled at her. "It could've been worse. The kitten could have knocked me on my ass. I remember a hellcat doing that to me once upon a time."

Lyric made a face at him. "I knock you on your butt *one* time, and I never hear the end of it."

"You do have one hell of a right hook," Billy chided her.

"And you have a glass jaw," Asp said as he came into the kitchen wearing his coat and carrying Billy's. Billy worked his good hand through the sleeve, and Asp slung the coat over his other shoulder. "Be back soon." Asp leaned down and kissed his wife.

"I have banana cream pie for dessert."

Both Billy and Asp groaned. "Man, you pick the absolute worst dinners to fuck up."

"I've only fucked up *this* one." They walked to the door.

"Which *is* the absolute worst." Asp made a face that said *idiot,* but his words didn't.

"Then stay and eat. I'm a big boy," Billy said as Asp closed the door behind them.

"Nope. Doc Cassidy isn't here. They went to Colorado to spend time with relatives."

Billy stopped and stared at the clinic. That was why the female doctor was there that morning. The one who looked like Mandy. Fuck. Today really wasn't his day. He turned to Asp. "You're shitting me, right. This is some kind of joke."

"I'm not, and it isn't. Lyric mentioned it tonight. Keelee said they'd be gone for three weeks, and I'm not going to let you go over there by yourself." Asp put a hand on his shoulder and pushed him forward. "Move it, Pearson, you need stitches."

"Fuck my life," Billy groaned and put one foot in front of the other.

They hit the buzzer, and the night nurse appeared to let them into the clinic. It was a security precaution that had started after the Siege. Those who came up from the underground facility didn't need to be buzzed in for access, but those who came from the outside were monitored.

"What happened?" the nurse asked as she took them back to an exam room.

"Murder kittens," Billy grumbled.

"Say what now?" The woman turned and frowned at him.

"An accident involving kittens." Billy shook his head. "They tried to kill me."

"They almost did," Asp agreed, but the laughter in his voice wasn't appreciated.

Billy glared at him, and when the nurse turned away, he flipped off his friend. That got Asp laughing for real.

"Take off your coat and sit there," the woman said, pointing to a white paper-lined exam table, and Billy complied. If he were lucky, the nurse would take care of him, and he'd escape without seeing Mandy's doppelganger.

The nurse carefully unwrapped the dishtowel. "Don't open your hand any more than it is," she commented as she cleaned around the cut. "All right. I'll ring the doctor, and you'll be stitched up and out of here in no time."

"You can't stitch it?" Even to his ears, his voice sounded a bit desperate.

The woman chuckled. "I could probably do a decent job, but I'm not a doctor. I'll be right back."

As the woman left, a man stepped into the doorway. "Asp."

"Malice." Asp walked over and extended his hand. "This guy is Billy."

Billy stood up and lifted his hand. "I'd offer to shake your hand, but …"

"Yeah, I'm good." Malice chuckled. "What happened?"

"Murder kittens." Asp laughed as he spoke.

Malice lifted his eyebrows. "Is that why your back is bloody?"

Billy snapped his head to look at his shoulder. Sure enough, where the murder kitten had attached itself was bloody. "Their freaking claws are like needles."

"And the hand?" Malice asked.

"Another of the lunatics jumped up onto the counter and sent the butcher knife flying. I caught the cat in one hand and the knife in the other." Billy shook his head. "All this because I wanted roast pork and all the fixings."

Malice leaned against the door frame. "You cooked that? Damn, that sounds good."

Asp snorted, "No, my wife did. There's more than enough, and she's keeping it warm for us. Join us after we get done here."

"Nah, thank you, though. My woman, Anya, is in the room down the hall. We've had some dinner."

"Did she tell you I came by this morning?" Billy asked.

Malice deadpanned, "She said something about a crazy person coming by, yes."

"That would be him." Asp pointed at him.

"Dude, I was just excited about talking to someone else in the profession. I get enough of you and Alex." He hadn't acted crazy. Well, not until the doctor came in.

"Stop by tomorrow morning after nine. She isn't sure what she can share and what she can't, so if I'm there, it would be better."

"Thanks, man. I'll stop by. I live downstairs, so I'll pop up." Hell yeah, he'd love to pick the little sniper's brain.

"She can't know about that. She doesn't have a clearance." Malice stood up and looked down the hall. "I'll get out of your way. Hey, Lillian."

"Malice, you didn't cut your hand, did you?"

Billy felt gut-punched when he heard that voice. Memories screamed in his mind as a tidal wave of thoughts he'd not so successfully buried surfaced.

"No, ma'am. That would be Billy and the murder kittens."

"The what?" The woman appeared in the doorway. "Oh, hello again."

Billy swallowed hard. The woman's hair was pulled up in a messy bun. She wore an old pair of jeans, a t-shirt that looked like it had been washed a thousand times, and a pair of fuzzy slippers. "What about murder kittens?" she asked as she walked into the exam room. The sound of her voice was a torment, so familiar yet different. Her words pulled him between the here and now and the memories he couldn't escape.

"Check out his back," Malice said from the doorway.

"I thought you were leaving?" Billy gave the guy a *thanks a lot* look.

Malice chuckled and lifted a hand. "Night, see you tomorrow."

Lillian looked up. "I'll check on Anya before I leave."

"Thanks, Lillian. I'll go say good night and head out." Malice drifted away from the doorway.

Billy jolted when the woman touched his hand. "Is it that painful?" Lillian lifted her eyes to his. Her gaze didn't waver. Her likeness to Mandy drove him into a bittersweet prison of his own making.

No, they weren't Mandy's eyes. But damn, it was a close thing.

"Billy?"

He jerked his head toward Asp. "What?"

"The doctor asked you if it hurt?"

"Oh. No, not really. It's a clean cut." He turned his attention back to the woman standing next to him. She was looking at the cut and putting on gloves. The emotions raging inside him clashed with her clinical detachment and professionalism. He drew a deep breath, trying to calm himself, and that was when he drew in the light floral scent of her perfume. It flitted past his senses, a haunting whisper of the present that mingled with the visions of his past. It wasn't the earthy kind that Mandy wore; it was light and delicate.

"This is a hard location. Every time you move your hand, the wound will pull." The nurse walked in with a tray covered with plastic. "Thank you, Cathy."

While the doctor set up, Billy looked over at Asp, who was staring at the doctor, too. When Asp finally looked over at him, Billy raised his eyebrows in question. Asp swallowed hard and nodded once. Their unspoken connection was a lifeline holding him steady as he walked the tightrope of his own disbelief. Asp had met Mandy. He knew, and that nod confirmed Billy wasn't insane. Knowing he wasn't going crazy helped more than he was willing to admit.

"All right, I'm going to numb this up. Small pinches." Billy returned his attention to the doctor as she worked. Her fingers were thin and capable, but Billy wasn't seeing what the doctor was doing. Instead, he was a lifetime away in a small apartment just outside base, listening to Mandy talk to him as she doctored the rope burns he'd gotten on the confidence course. Every touch was a mirror image of that tenderness and a ghost of the comfort he'd thrown away.

"Why don't you use gloves?"

"Because when you're deployed, you might not have time to find a pair when you need to climb a rope." The blisters would harden, and the skin under would toughen up, but Mandy liked to fuss over him.

"I'm buying you a pair for every set of BDUs you own." She looked at him. Her beautiful green eyes were wide with worry. There was a spattering of freckles over her nose, which just made her all the more beautiful.

"You don't need to do that. I'm fine. I was in a hurry and slipped. It won't happen again."

She soothed the ointment on the palm of his hand. It

would do nothing but extend the time needed for the skin under the blister to harden, but he didn't care.

"There's a date night at the club on Friday night. Two for one prime rib. Crystal told me about it. Should I make a reservation?"

The NCO club was the hub of their small community. "Sure." Mandy put the cap on the ointment, and he caught her with his good hand. "But for us. I want you all to myself before we deploy. We can double date with Crystal and Doogie when we get back."

Mandy smiled and draped her arms over his neck. "It's Doug."

"Dougie, Doogie, whatever." Billy laughed when she couldn't hide her smile.

She glanced back at him. "It's just three months this time, right?"

"Three to six, but the brass is saying less than six." He kissed her full, soft lips.

She sighed and leaned into him. "I hope it's less. I want you here when the baby is born."

"Come hell or high water." He leaned down and kissed her belly. "I'll be here and wearing a catcher's mitt, just in case the doctor misses catching my kid. Gotta have backup."

Mandy laughed and spun away. "This little angel is not going to be caught in a catcher's mitt."

"Why not? Think of the story she'd have to tell. Besides, it could be a he, and then, boom, instant karma. A major leaguer for sure." Billy followed his fiancée from the bathroom to the kitchen. "You know I can get us an appointment with the judge. We can get married before I leave."

Mandy turned around and crossed her arms. "I've always wanted a wedding with a white gown and a three-tier cake. Mom and Dad didn't leave me much, but I have enough for that. After this little one is born and I have my figure back, I'll make an honest man out of you."

Billy laughed and swaggered across the floor until he was all up in her space. "Well, then, if you won't marry me, why don't we practice making babies again?"

"Because we already know how to do that. Obviously." Mandy wrapped her arms around his neck. The laughter in her eyes was one of the first things that had attracted him to her.

"But, baby, we can't forget how to do it. It would be horrible to have to fumble and bumble about trying to remember what goes where." Billy rotated his hips against her.

"Well, then, maybe you should remind me once or twice."

Billy swung her up into his arms, and she shrieked,

grabbing around his neck and laughing as he trotted down the small hallway to their bedroom.

Asp's hand on his shoulder made him jump. He glanced down at his hand. The doctor was bandaging it. "There you go." She looked up at him. "You're pale. Do you have a thing about seeing your own blood? I've known a few guys who could wade through a river of the stuff, but if they saw their own, they'd drop like a rock."

Billy shook his head. "No. I'm good."

"Okay, I'm assuming you know the drill. Keep it dry until it closes completely. Come back in ten days, and I'll take the sutures out. Hold on while I call up your chart."

There was no way he was coming back to have her take out the stitches. He had a pair of scissors and some tweezers.

The woman walked over to the computer in the room and woke it up. She glanced at the tablet the nurse had jotted his information down on, then at the computer. "You're up to date on your tetanus."

"Is that even a thing anymore?" Asp asked as he walked toward the coat rack where Billy had deposited his coat.

"You'd be surprised," the woman said in a non-committal way. "Billy Pearson." She turned and smiled at him. "A pleasure to meet formally. In case you didn't catch my name this morning, I'm Lillian Montrose."

Billy nodded as Asp stepped in front of him, breaking his eye contact with the doctor, and handed him his coat. "I'm sorry. I should have introduced myself earlier," Asp said, turning around and extending his hand. "Isaac Cooper. I work with Guardian, as does Billy, which you know because you have his records."

Billy stood and put on his coat, gently sliding his hand through the sleeve. He was grateful for Asp running interference. Asp wasn't the gregarious type. He didn't talk just to make noise, and there he was, sucking that up and keeping the doctor occupied. His friend was aces in his book.

"I'm ready," Billy said from behind Asp.

"About time. I'm starving." Asp nodded at the doctor. "Night, good to meet you."

Billy nodded as he walked out of the exam room. The nurse went into the room as they turned down the hallway. "I'm going to head downstairs," Billy said as they reached the T in the hallway. "Tell Lyric I'll be back when the murder kittens have been rehomed."

Asp paused beside him. "You zoned out hard in there. Are you okay?"

"Yeah. Just remembering her. Vivid shit." Billy tried to give him a smile. "I'll go downstairs, pick up a sandwich from the kitchen, have a beer, watch a mindless movie, and then get some sleep. It's been one hell of a day."

"Do you need to talk to Doc Wheeler?" Asp mentioned the shrink in Hollister.

Billy pushed out a surprised laugh. "No. I'm not mental. You saw her. She looks just like Mandy, doesn't she?"

"I see the resemblance, but there's quite a difference. The eyes are all wrong, and she's taller. Something about her cheeks or maybe her nose is different, but yeah, I can see why you had a shock." Asp crossed his arms. "But, dude, she's *not* Mandy."

Billy rolled his eyes. "No shit. Mandy is finally happy and has a family." One that didn't involve him. He'd brought nothing but death and pain into Mandy's life. She was better off without him. "As I said, I'm not mental. I don't plan on getting drunk. I worked through all the surprise feelings she brought up at the firing range. The sound of bullets hitting the target is my therapy of choice."

"All right. I'll see you tomorrow. Let me know

when you come up to talk to Anya. I'd like to hear what she has to say."

"Will do." Billy turned to walk away but stopped. He turned around, and Asp was still in the same place he'd been standing. "Thanks, by the way. For coming and turning into a social butterfly back there."

Asp sighed and turned to him. "I'm going to say this again. You should go see Jeremiah Wheeler. I saw the resemblance, Billy, but …"

"You think I have issues?"

"I think you need to talk to someone. Your reaction …" Asp nodded as he spoke. "Please."

Billy was so messed up that the plea from his friend about broke him. "I'll call him." What the fuck could it hurt?

"Whatever it takes, my friend."

"For as long as it takes." Billy turned and headed down the hallway to the supply closet and the nearest elevator down to the underground facility. He hit the button to close the door and drew a deep breath. What a fucking day.

CHAPTER 4

"You did what? Could you repeat that?" Dr. Wheeler asked him.

"I went to Kentucky to see her. That's why I rescheduled from last week." Billy studied the toe of his boot, not looking at the doctor. "I knew it was stupid, but I needed to see her again."

"All right. Tell me why you needed to see her, especially if seeing you would open wounds for her she's evidently healed from?"

Billy glanced up at him and frowned. "Well, don't sugarcoat the questions or anything."

"I could, but it would be a waste of my time and yours. Tell me why you had to go." Doc Wheeler leaned back in his chair and crossed his cowboy boots while staring at him.

"I had to make sure."

"Of what?"

Billy dropped his head back on the big chair and sighed. "That she was happy."

"Right. You know she's married and has a family. So, what was the real reason?" The doctor pushed him for an answer.

Billy shrugged. "Maybe ... Hell, Doc, how did *she* move on when *I* can't?"

"Ah." Dr. Wheeler nodded. "You can't move on from her, or perhaps you just can't move on."

Billy snapped his head in the doctor's direction. "What? What does that mean?"

"Have you dated?"

"Thought about it. I talked to some women, locals here, but if I need to get some physical release, I know where to go, so there aren't any attachments."

"Attachments are an issue for you?" the doctor prodded.

"No." Billy shook his head. "I have good friends here in town and on the ranch."

The doctor nodded. "Male friends."

"Lyric is a friend, and she's definitely not a

male." The little hellcat was as feisty as they came, and she'd become a good friend.

"True, but she's safe. She's married."

Billy felt his defenses go up and tried to quash the feeling. It didn't work. "I don't understand the point you're trying to make, Doc."

"Why do you think you haven't dated?"

"Well, for the first handful of years, I was working for what I thought was the CIA. There wasn't any time. Then, after Guardian cleared me and took me on, I was learning my place in the organization." He'd been busy. The doctor knew that.

Doc Wheeler nodded. "Let's look at it another way. How did you feel when you saw the pictures of Mandy? The ones the CIA showed you?"

"Pissed." Billy shot the word back at him. "Then cornered." He leaned forward and dropped his elbows to his knees. "Then … guilty as fuck. I did that to her, Doc. My service and my recruitment caused the loss of our baby, and I caused her to break down. *Fuck,*" he hissed.

"And that's where you've stayed. Feeling guilty."

Billy stood up and walked to the huge ocean painting in the office. "Wouldn't you?"

"We aren't talking about me," Doc Wheeler said.

"Did you cause the incident where you were injured?"

"No." Billy shook his head and turned around to look at the doctor. "No, I didn't cause the incident. I wasn't responsible for what the military or the CIA did with the notifications, but I sure as fuck was responsible for staying and working for the CIA. I could have gone back. But I didn't."

"Why?"

"Because I *couldn't*." Billy ran his hands through his hair. "She lost the baby."

"Did you love Mandy?" Doc Wheeler asked quietly.

Billy looked down at the floor and stared at the seam running between the floorboards. "We were going to get married."

"That's not what I asked."

"Fuck." Billy swore again. "*I could have*. I could have been a good husband and father."

"Why did you ask her to marry you? Was it because of the baby?"

Billy nodded. "We would have gotten there eventually. I really cared for her. But we'd only been together for a year, and most of that time, I was deployed."

"How many months were you deployed?"

"I don't know, five, maybe six?"

"And while you cared for her, you knew you weren't in love."

Billy nodded. "But I would have been there for her and the baby. I'd have done the best by them."

"I'm sure you would have." Doc Wheeler was silent for a moment before asking, "Losing the child released you from your duty to Mandy, didn't it?"

"That's what I told myself. She'd be better off without me." Billy sniffed and wiped at his eyes. "Fuck, I'm dripping."

"It happens," Doc Wheeler said. "Come sit down, Billy."

He did and stared at the doctor. "I'm a piece of shit."

The doctor shook his head. "No, you're human." He leaned forward. "According to Guardian's records, you deposited money into her account every month while you were with the CIA. Why?"

"I had to take care of her. I had the CIA draft up a letter and tell her the money was from a life insurance policy I had set up for her, and it would be paid monthly until it ran out."

"Do you still pay her?"

Billy shook his head.

"Why?"

"She's married, and he's doing well." Billy looked directly at the doctor. "I still feel guilty for abandoning her."

"What is it going to take to forgive yourself?"

"Huh?" *Forgive himself? Hell, how could he do that?*

"You've paid for your decision, Billy. You've paid. The guilt that has consumed you is misplaced. You made a decision when you were emotionally and physically damaged. That's a recruitment tactic. You were placed in that position. You didn't volunteer to be there. If you hadn't been hurt, you would have gone home and married a woman you hoped to love one day. You would have been a father, or maybe not. No one knows if the baby would have gone to full term. No one knows what tomorrow holds, Billy. You've played out the scenario in your head, so you have a perfect picture of how things *should have* unfolded for you and for Mandy. But she still would have been notified of your death. She still would have lost the baby, and she would have ended up in treatment. All that happened before you woke up in that hospital. The CIA preyed on that mistake. You chose to not go back, yet you ensured she was cared for. *Own that.* You made a choice based on what was best for *you and for her.* You knew somewhere deep inside that you didn't love her how she needed to be loved. Your decision and how you cared for her financially gave her the opportunity to have the life she has now."

Billy stared at the doctor as the blocks seemed to fall into place. Of course, he knew what Doc Wheeler said was true. He closed his eyes. "That doesn't make what I did easier to live with."

"Probably not." The doctor nodded. "But then again, how about we get you to a point where you actually start living and deal with it as we go?"

"And what will that entail?" Billy stared at the man across from him.

"Ah, some uncomfortable work from you and some visits here. Are you ready for your first round of homework?"

Billy stared at the doctor. "Why do I get the feeling I'm not going to like you too much by the time we're done?"

Doc Wheeler chuckled. "Reserve your judgment for a couple of months, okay?"

Billy lifted an eyebrow. "If I have to."

"You do. Now, let's talk about that homework."

CHAPTER 5

T*wo months later*:

Lillian made her way to the conference room in the underground facility. Adam Cassidy met her at the door. As she entered, she noticed the video feed up in the room with several dividers. It was currently blank, making the screen look like a windowpane. "What's up?" she greeted.

"I don't know. Mike just said we had a conference call. Hopefully, they won't pull you away. I'm having too much fun being lazy."

"Lazy? Is that what you call the crazy workouts you do outside?"

"That's a habit. I've been working out every day with Double D and Mike for as long as I can remember. When the temperature is above freezing, we take advantage of the nice weather," Adam said as he walked in behind her. "The laziness is not having a call when the clinic is closed. You'd be surprised how many people hurt themselves at night around here."

"I've only had a handful. Burns, cuts, a twisted ankle ... oh, and the occasional foot squishing from horses. Now that Anya's been discharged, I've been doing some research and reading. I'm really enjoying the downtime." Lillian laughed.

"I can imagine. I bet a Mercy Team is a big step down in pace from your infectious disease work." Adam pulled out a chair for her, which was something she noticed about all the men around there. They were polite, and their manners were impeccable. Well, with the exception of one Billy Pearson, who would do an about-face if he saw her walking in the same direction as him. It was the weirdest thing, but she decided to follow Abe's counsel and let the man own his issues.

"Thank you. And I was so glad Guardian offered me the job. I know Abe's brother Cash had a lot to do with referring both Abe and me, but the Mercy Team work has been rewarding and still allows us to work as temps in the hospital system when we're not deployed." Research was her first love, but she couldn't go on in that capacity. Still, give her a puzzle, and she was immediately happy. She'd completed medical school, an internal medicine residency, and an infectious disease fellowship. Following her Infectious Disease Board certification, she'd started work with Plume Laboratories. That was where she'd met Dion. Dion the Dick, as Abe called him.

Mike White Cloud walked in and shut the door. "Lillian, Adam. Are you ready?"

"For what?" Adam asked, leaning forward.

"Don't know. Archangel asked for the meeting. Hold on, let me get everyone onboard before I call in the big guy." Mike sat down, picked up a tablet off the table, and within a few seconds, several cameras turned on. Mike unmuted everyone.

"What's up, Jewell?" Lillian waved at Jewell, whom she'd met via video conferences several times when she was being hired.

"Hey! How are you liking South Dakota?" Jewell leaned back and smiled at her.

"It's cold, but I'm loving the time to recharge." She felt like a different person.

"All right, we're all on. CCS, bring in Archangel, please." Mike said when all but one screen populated.

"Hold." Jewell moved forward, and Lillian heard her keyboard clacking. The last square on the screen populated.

"Mike, is everyone here?" Archangel asked in the way of a greeting.

"Affirmative. We have Alpha, Fury, CCS, Doc Cassidy, Doc Montrose, and Anubis on via video." Lillian's eyes darted from frame to frame as Mike went through the call signs. She knew Kaden, or Anubis, as he was called by Guardian, was usually in the underground facility, but it looked like he was elsewhere today.

"All connections are secure," Jewell said after Mike finished.

"All right. I imagine you're wondering what's going on, so I'll cut to the chase. Dr. Montrose, is it possible that a drug, a hallucinogenic or perhaps a poison, can be engineered to be spread by skin-to-skin contact, such as a handshake?"

Lillian jerked at the question. "Yes, absolutely. The carrier would either be inoculated or sacrificed with the intent of spreading the disease or contagion."

Archangel took off his glasses and looked at the camera. "That's what our research confirmed, too." He sighed. "We have credible information there are plans to disrupt the International Peace Summit the United States and France are backing and hosting. One of the lines of reasoning that has been repeatedly heard but not verified by any organization is the threat of such an event at the summit."

"Three months out, and rumors are flying? Either it's misdirection, or whoever is planning it is shit at keeping their people quiet."

Lillian nodded and agreed with Fury. "There has never been a mass exposure of this nature in environments that weren't enclosed. Typically, an air or water-borne pathogen would create such a threat. I've never been to a summit, but I'm assuming the security would be intense. I can't imagine a drug or poison that could be passed in such a way it wouldn't diminish as it was passed along. Imagine having chalk on your hand. As you shake a person's hand, what you have on your hand is diminished, and it goes on and on. Granted, there could be widespread contact, but the amount being spread would soon be negligible."

"Unless it's so potent, it only takes a small amount," Anubis interrupted. "I've worked with poisons. It's possible."

Adam nodded. “Carfentanil and fentanyl come to mind.”

“Carfentanil?” Jewell asked.

“Elephant tranquilizer,” Lillian supplied. “Ten thousand times more powerful than morphine and a hundred times more potent than fentanyl.”

Alpha leaned forward. “But could a carrier survive that much contact?”

“Not with that type of drug.” Adam shrugged. “Until you know what you’re dealing with, it’s a crap shoot.”

“Exactly.” Archangel nodded. “That’s why I want Mercy Teams Three, Four, Five, and Six to converge on the annex and use the classrooms aboveground to go over possible scenarios. We need to procure and stockpile equipment and known antidotes, such as Narcan, in the case of fentanyl, to prepare for the summit. All four teams will deploy to the summit, and each will have the equipment and medication with them. Fury and Alpha, you will assign an overwatch for each of the teams. I want them protected. Use all available resources. Charlie, Delta, and Echo teams will be deployed to provide security and respond if needed. The overwatches will work under Charlie Team’s leader but are independently authorized to act should the need arise. The French government is welcoming our participation. Other countries will be working on measures to further protect the participants. The stabilization of the Middle East depends on this meeting and those peace accords being signed. The president has expressed his grave concerns over the rumors."

"But they're unsubstantiated," Fury said again.

"Unverified, but that doesn't mean unintentional," Alpha said. "Don't forget about the lessons we learned from the 2020 coup d'état in Africa. The government used this very tactic to undermine its political adversaries. They floated the rumors of a coup for so long that after a couple of months with no action, no one took it as an actual threat."

"Which is a damn good point," Archangel said. "If this never materializes, then we've conducted a drill and learned lessons. Mike, you're in charge of getting the Mercy Teams whatever they need, plus coordinating the transportation of the teams to the annex. Anubis, do you have enough lodging in the aboveground facility to accommodate them?"

"Two per team?" Anubis asked.

"Correct, plus overwatches and Alpha's teams. However, some of them will have the clearance to live in the underground facility. I want these people to know each other, so the teams and overwatches will notice if something's wrong," Archangel ordered.

"Roger that. We're good. Some might have to double-bunk, but we'll get them sorted. I'll work with Mike on it," Anubis confirmed.

"Lillian, I'm putting you in charge of the Mercy Teams for this show. We'll be leaning hard on your background in infectious disease. Alpha, I need you to go to the Annex and work with not only the teams, but also the Mercy Teams and overwatches. I'll get you the maps for the summit, the buildings being used, and the underground services and tunnels. You develop a plan for the deployment of our teams. Adam, because of your background on combat teams, if you see something Lillian isn't taking into consideration, you make sure both she and Alpha know about it. Does anyone have any questions?"

"Comms on the ground at the Summit?" CCS asked when no one else spoke up.

"We'll be tapped into the French government's system, but I want redundancy. Have Mercy Team and the overwatches fitted for our comm systems so they can communicate with whoever is controlling the European node at the time."

"Righto, that's what I was hoping for," Jewell said as she typed.

"Anyone else?" Archangel looked up at the screen.

"How many units are we looking to stockpile? What's the population size we're looking to protect?" Lillian needed an idea of how much medication she'd need. The storage of each would be specific.

"Delegates and entourages directly involved in the summit. Five hundred. That's more than will be attending, so you'll have a cushion should something happen to prevent one of the teams from responding."

Lillian nodded, but Archangel's comment sent her mind reeling. *What would prevent a medical team from responding?*

She had to physically shake her head to clear the thought and tune back into what Archangel was saying. "We'll meet weekly until we deploy. Hopefully, this is just an exercise in caution, but we need to prepare like we're going to war. Are we clear?"

Lillian watched as everyone nodded. Mike

cleared them, then turned to her and Adam. "I'll be available for whatever you need."

Adam leaned forward, looking at Lillian. "I'll look at your notes when you want me to, but I'm going to stay out of your way on the infectious side of the house. That'll be your baby."

She sighed and nodded. "All this is a bit over my head. I worked in infectious disease research. HIV, the explosion of antibiotic-resistant infections. I did clinical research. This, the real-world guesswork, is going to be the biggest puzzle I've ever attempted." Her brain was racing with the scope of what she'd been tasked to do.

"Well, if you want my input, I'd say stick to the basics. In chemical warfare, we have Atropine and Pralidoxime, which are readily available as an antidote. For nerve agents, we have Diazepam if they're seizing. Airborne chemicals on the skin would be immediate decontamination, so request those types of stations to be set up."

Lillian nodded. "Yeah, and then we have things like Anthrax and Botulinum toxin, which we can get vaccinations for. But we'd need to consider the others. Ricin and VX, plus Sarin, will always be a concern. For the most part, they're odorless, tasteless, and colorless. It's a bitch to detect, easy to spread. Each team will have to know the symptoms of each toxin and the best treatment when they're in doubt. Some of the antidotes don't like each other, and mixing them could be fatal."

"Education. We have three months and damn smart people. You'll manage," Adam reassured her.

Lillian nodded, knowing it but glad to hear the words said out loud. She moved on to the next concern. "The proper storage could be an issue."

"No. Just tell me what you need. We can get portable refrigeration units and smaller packs to deploy with the team," Mike said. "Money isn't an object. Tell me what you need, and I'll get it or have it made."

Lillian was impressed. "I'll do that. Right now, I need to find a notebook and get these thoughts down on paper."

"Ah, old school. A woman after our hearts." Adam chuckled.

"Nope, not at all. I've met your wives. I'm not after anything." Lillian laughed and stood up. "Except for a tablet and a pen."

"I can help with that." Mike walked over to a credenza under the huge monitor they'd just been staring at and pulled open a drawer. "Here you go." He handed her a legal pad and two pens.

"Perfect. Can I stay here and jot all this down?" She looked at Mike.

"You bet. Stay as long as you want. Shae and I need to start a recall and work travel arrangements for the other Mercy Teams."

"Oh, crap," Lillian said.

"What's wrong?" Adam frowned and stopped his walk to the door.

"Nothing, really. My teammate, Abe, returned from his honeymoon a little over a month ago, and they're in the process of moving into their house." She grimaced. Heather would be so pissed. "Can you give him some time? He's worked in infectious disease as long as I have, and I won't have to bring him up to speed on the majority of this."

Chief nodded. "I'll have to clear it with the bosses, but I don't see that being a problem."

"Oh, good." She sighed, blowing out a long breath. "Now, on to dumping my brain onto paper."

"If you need anything, you know how to reach us," Mike said from the door.

Lillian heard him but was already writing things down. She worked through one pen and chucked it in the trash can.

Her stomach growled for the fifth or sixth time

as she reviewed what she'd written. She'd finished off one legal tablet and pulled another out of the credenza hours ago. Lillian glanced up at the clock and then flashed a look at her watch. Eight hours? No wonder her stomach was complaining. She went through her notes one more time, looking for obvious holes in her thought process. Her stomach growled again. Standing, she grabbed the tablets and put one under her arm while reading the other. She looked up enough to get out of the conference room, then headed down the long hallway that would take her to the cafeteria. She popped the pen into her teeth and flipped the page backward in the tablet.

CHAPTER 6

Lillian mumbled around the pen, "I know I accounted for that." *Didn't I?* Lillian walked on and flipped another page back. Which, in hindsight, was her first mistake. She collided and then bounced off an immovable object, landing on her ass after an inelegant and sprawling fall to the floor.

"Shit," a man said.

Lillian looked up from the spray of yellow paper to the owner of that voice. Her heart skipped a beat in her chest, then started doing flips—a reaction she couldn't control. *Oh, great.*

"Are you okay?" One Billy Pearson leaned over her and extended his hand.

"Oh, so you can talk." She disregarded his

hand. "Thanks, but no thanks. Your sudden realization I exist is as startling as it is unnecessary. I wouldn't want to spread cooties to you or something." Lillian rolled onto her knees and picked up her notes before crawling four feet to retrieve her pen. She stood up and turned back toward the cafeteria. "Why are you still here?"

"Did you say cooties?" A half-assed smile seemed to form momentarily on the man's face.

"Probably," she admitted. She hated that her voice carried a mix of irritation and a healthy dose of involuntary curiosity. She wasn't curious about the man. Nope. Not at all. "Excuse me." She made a move around him.

"I don't think you have cooties," he said from behind her.

"Could've fooled me." She used the words like a shield because she refused to admit she felt a flutter in her chest when he talked to her. She didn't even look up from her notes to respond to him but did manage to turn into the cafeteria about twenty feet farther down the hall. The lights came on automatically when she entered. Lillian slowly meandered back to the refrigerator area. That was where the food for the residents who couldn't make it to a scheduled meal up above was stored.

Lillian stood in front of the fridge, reading her notes.

"Are you getting something?"

"Shit!" She jumped and spun. Mr. Pearson was right behind her. "Are you following me?"

"Ah … yes and no. I was coming to get something to eat." He motioned to the huge silver refrigeration unit behind her.

"Oh." Her response softened, and she felt a reluctant awareness of his nearness. She stepped back and dropped her eyes to her notes, pretending to not notice how handsome he was. Because she definitely didn't notice that perfect smile, those muscled arms and shoulders, or the narrow waist where his t-shirt was tucked. She peeked up as he opened the door to the fridge. Or that tight cute ass. *Lord above, she did* not *just think that. Get a grip, woman.*

But she had, and that was so out of her normal thought pattern. The man in front of her bent over and reached into the unit. Lillian felt her eyes bug out and dropped her gaze immediately as she felt a rush of heat to her cheeks. It was just like a high school crush, ridiculous and untimely. No, she wasn't doing this. She *obviously* had a blood sugar issue going on. She missed lunch and dinner. No wonder she was having weird thoughts.

"Looks like they have sub sandwiches or a heat-and-go plate of roast beef and mashed potatoes."

Lillian looked up and then looked around the room that was vacant except for the two of them. "Are you talking to me?" She pointed to herself.

Billy dropped his head and shut the door to the refrigeration unit. "Look." He sighed as if the weight of his past actions were bearing down on him. "When we first met, I acted kind of out there."

Well, *now* he had her attention. She stiffened. "Rude. I'd call it rude, not 'out there.'" Her voice was steady with resolve that time. One thing she'd learned in therapy after Dion the Dick was to speak her truth and not let anyone dissuade her of its importance or accuracy.

"Fair enough. There's a reason behind all of that. Have dinner with me, and I'll explain." The guy crossed his arms and shrugged.

"No." She shook her head. She wouldn't get sucked in again.

"No?" The shocked look on his face was almost comical. "Why not?"

"Because I haven't heard an apology. I've heard

excuses, minimalization, and rationalization, and believe me, I don't have the time or the inclination to deal with another gaslighting narcissist."

The man blinked at her and then blinked again. "Okay, there's so much to unpack right there, but let me start by saying I'm sorry. I'm sorry for acting like a jerk, being rude, and knocking you into next week just now. I'm sorry for avoiding you like you had cooties." And now, he sounded sincere. Damn it, he was getting past her defenses. She could see the fortress walls starting to crumble. That smile spread across his face again. "Cooties is a medical term, right?"

She stared at him for a moment, during which she waged a silent war with herself. Did she stay guarded, or did she walk through the open door of his apology? She sighed. *Hello, door.* "A highly technical term, yes." She couldn't hide the smile that played on her lips. "I accept your apology."

"Thank you. Would you like to have a meal with me and listen to why I was acting like such a …"

"Douche?" she supplied.

He winced a little too dramatically, "Ouch, but okay, I probably earned that."

"You did." Her response was firm, but there was

also a tinge of humor that hadn't been there before. She called it how she saw it.

Billy rolled his eyes. "Then I'll own it. Sandwiches or hot plate?"

"I'll have a sandwich, please. Turkey if they have it." Lillian watched him pull out two sandwiches and drop them on a tray.

"Chips or salad?"

"Salad, please. No dressing." She dropped her paper and pen onto a table close by and headed to the beverage area. After washing her hands, she picked up two glasses. "Do you want water or a soft drink?"

He looked over at her. "Coke, please."

She poured water for herself and a soft drink for him, then took them back to the table, along with a small stack of napkins and two utensil bundles.

They unwrapped their sandwiches in silence, and she waited until he took a bite. "So, you were going to explain your douchiness." She stabbed at her salad with her fork.

He nodded as he chewed. "You remind me of someone," he said as he opened his bag of chips.

She leveled an examining glare at him. "And?" She was skeptical he'd be able to explain his actions based on that bit of information, and she wouldn't let herself be vulnerable in any way with him until she had a complete reason for his actions. She wouldn't let him get off the hook that damn easily.

He sighed and moved to take his wallet out of his back pocket. He opened it and looked at the inside of his wallet for a moment before pulling out a picture. "This is Mandy. We were engaged."

Lillian wiped off her fingers and took the old photograph from him. She turned it toward herself and stared at an image that could have been her sister if she had one. She narrowed her eyes and stared at the likeness in the photograph. There was a similarity, but they definitely weren't twins. His picture seemed to span the gap between them, connecting his past to their present, but there had to be more than an old photo. Lillian was taller and curvier than the woman. Their hair was different, and so was the shape of their face. She had higher cheekbones, and her chin wasn't as defined as the woman's. But she could see why Billy thought they looked similar. "You said you were engaged?" She was respectful and hesitant to ask the question in case she unknowingly wandered onto sacred ground. She handed the photo back to him.

"Yeah. A lot of things happened, and the military told her I'd died. She miscarried our baby and was committed to an institution for treatment." His voice caught on the last word, and she could hear the pain that accompanied their loss and her treatment. He took the picture back from her. "She lost so much because of me." Lillian looked up at the man. She heard something else. Something she'd learned to identify quickly. He felt guilty. He said nothing for a moment before continuing, "You sound a bit like her, too. The same husky quality in your voice. It was such a shock; it threw me for a loop or two. Or twenty. I went into defensive mode when I saw you. I was trying to shield myself from everything I'd buried. I hadn't dealt with a lot of the baggage that event caused. So, I acted like a dick. Again, I'm sorry for that."

"Where is she now?" Lillian took a bite of her sandwich as questions crowded her brain. The questions swarmed like wasps, stinging with their need to be answered. Questions she didn't have the right to ask but wanted to know, like why in the hell wasn't he with her? How did the military make such a heinous mistake? What type of hell did he go through when he found out she'd lost the baby and been committed?

"She's in Kentucky. Married with a family. I went back there after I saw you. I had to reassure myself she was happy."

Lillian stared at the man, and a realization developed rather quickly. As a matter of fact, it hit with the force of a speeding freight train. "She still doesn't know you're alive, does she?"

* * *

BILLY SHOOK HIS HEAD. Years of guilt still weighed him down. He'd needed to have that conversation with Lillian. Not only was it the right thing to do, but it was a homework assignment. When he knocked her on her ass, he figured there was no time like the present. But fuck, the present sucked. Talk about a festering pit of regret and what-ifs. "No. She doesn't. There was a period of years after I was reported as dead that I worked for a ... cloaked organization." He tried to not make it sound like he was keeping secrets, but the darkness of what he'd done wasn't open for discussion. He wagged his head. That wasn't technically a lie, so he'd roll with it. Jeremiah could deal with the small fib. "After that, she'd already met someone. She was pregnant with their first baby. A boy. What good would it have done for me to show up? She was finally moving forward."

"But you haven't." Lillian stared at him. Her gaze pierced him as if she could see through his words to his soul.

"Damn, you should have been a prosecutor or a shrink, you know? Tough questions."

"That was an observation, not a question."

He laughed a bit but cleared his throat. "Which proves my point. Yeah, but to get back to it … I thought I'd buried it deep enough it didn't matter. Seeing you prompted me to get some help with that. For all intents and purposes, I'm a ghost in her life, and she's a ghost in mine. We're both alive but dead to each other."

Lillian lowered her eyes and took a bite of her salad. He ate the sawdust that was on his bread and waited for another question. "What do you do for Guardian?"

And that wasn't what he expected. "That's it? No more questions about Mandy?"

Lillian picked up her sandwich. "No. It sounds like a tragedy you don't need to pull out and examine again. At least not with me." Her voice was kind and gentle, offering him an out he didn't know he needed. She took a bite and looked at him expectantly.

"Oh, well, thanks for that. I'm a marksman. I teach it and deploy when needed. You?"

She finished eating and took a drink of water. "Team Leader for a Mercy Team. I'm currently stationed on the West Coast."

"And you came to South Dakota because of Anya?" He took a sip of his soft drink.

"Yes and no. My teammate got married. He's doing the honeymoon, move into a house thing. He took four months off, so Adam Cassidy suggested I come out and fill in for him while he visited his family. Anya just sped the transportation up by a couple days." Her explanation was factual, but her voice softened when she talked about her teammate. Billy detected a hint of loneliness. "I've been doing some professional reading, catching up on developments in my old career field, and filling in for him two days a week, so it was a win/win for both Adam and me."

"Is that what this is? Professional reading?" Billy nodded to the two tablets she'd placed face down on the table.

"Ah, no. That's a new mission that just came

down the pipe today." She shrugged, but her eyes glinted as if she were thrilled by the challenge. "Hell of a puzzle."

"You have many puzzles on Mercy Teams?"

"Not usually." She chuckled. The warmth of her laughter was a stark difference to the cool detachment of her initial comments to him. "But ..." She shrugged.

They sat in silence while he ate and examined her, hopefully covertly. She was similar to Mandy, but there were enough differences he could now see, especially after going back to Kentucky to check on Mandy. He was within ten feet of his ex-fiancée, her husband, and their son. The years had been kind, but in truth, Mandy *was* physically different than Lillian, and those differences were easier to see than before. While there were similarities, the mirage that overwhelmingly convicted him of his shame now faded with the light of his recent work with Dr. Wheeler. The shock that had made the two women seem like mirror images had fled.

"Did you take out your own stitches?" Lillian asked after she took a drink of water.

Billy snorted. "Yeah, about a week or so after I sliced it. Not the first time and probably not the last." He lifted his hand and spread it out so she could see her handiwork.

She glanced at his hand and lifted an eyebrow. "And the kittens that attempted your murder?"

"Man, you have a good memory, don't you?"

"Not many kitten murderers around here. Horses like to crush feet. Ice causes slips and falls. But I've had no repeat attempted murder by kitten."

Billy laughed. "She kept one, but the other two found homes."

"She?" Lillian asked.

"Isaac's wife. Isaac and I have been a team for a lifetime ... or two."

Lillian cocked her head. "There's a story there."

"More than one," Billy admitted. He drew a breath and decided to make a hell of a stretch. Get out of his comfort zone, as Doc Wheeler would say. "Hey, would you like to go to lunch with me? I can tell you a story or two on the way there and back."

"Why not now?" Lillian leaned back and spread her hands, indicating the table in front of them. "This is lunch and dinner for me."

Damn, she wouldn't make it easy for him, would she. Well, he'd jumped, so he'd sink or swim. "No, I mean, go into Hollister and grab something at the diner. Maybe a drink at the Bit and Spur."

"Hollister? How far is that?" Lillian took a sip of water.

He frowned as he put two and two together. "Wait, you haven't been off the ranch?"

She shook her head. "No. I've had no need to go anywhere."

"Okay, first, that's just anti-social. Second, the food at the diner is good."

"And third?"

Billy cocked his head. "You could use a drink."

She countered, "I have wine in my room."

Oh, man, she was a tough nut, wasn't she? Her verbal banter was engaging, though. "Drinking alone? Isn't that a sign of something?" Billy egged her on with a smile.

She angled her head and peered up at him. "Absolutely. It's a sign of being comfortable with oneself."

He laughed. Damn, he liked battling words with the woman. But … Billy lifted a finger. "Which reminds me, who was the gaslighting narcissistic son of a bitch who hurt you?"

She wiped her mouth and lifted her water glass

before sitting back in her chair. "Also a ghost. He's dead to me and a chapter of my life I try to not go back to."

Billy lifted his glass and held it halfway across the table. "Here's hoping all our ghosts stay where they belong."

She clicked her glass with his, took a sip, then said, "Yes."

He blinked at her. "Yes?"

She leveled a stare at him. "I'd like to go to Hollister sometime and have lunch and maybe a drink with you. As friends."

Billy chortled, "Well, I'd hate to go as enemies." God, it was fun to banter with her.

Lillian rolled her eyes. "I believe you know what I mean."

"I do. I wasn't looking for anything else." He started to put his wrapping on his tray.

"Especially with me." She wrapped up half her sandwich she hadn't eaten and put it on top of her legal pads.

"Why do you say that?" Billy stood up and walked to the trash with the tray.

"One, I'm not staying here past the extent of the mission I was just given. Two, I resemble someone from your past who caused a pretty significant emotional toll on you, and three, I've learned I'm important enough to me to not get involved with every attractive man who asks me out."

Billy smiled wide. "You think I'm attractive? Right back at you, Doc." He winked.

"Because I look like your Mandy." The doctor picked up her notebooks, pen, and the remainder of her sandwich.

"No, because you're sharp-witted and fun to talk with. Your resemblance to her was my problem, and as you saw with the picture, it wasn't as striking as I originally thought. As I said, that time in my life was baggage I needed to deal with, and I have … I am." He was working damn hard at unpacking all the shit that event had loaded on top of him, and even though it was harder than hell, he could see the bottom of the steamer trunk of issues he'd been carrying around. "How about Friday at about noon? I'll knock on your door, and we can head up."

"That sounds good, but if I'm not in my apartment, check in the conference room. The one with the glass table. I was able to get a good amount of work done there, and I might go back, depending on how the week goes."

"One hell of a mission, then?"

She sighed. "I really hope not, but we're going to prepare for the worst."

"And pray for the best." Billy finished for her. "A good motto."

Lillian chuckled, and they walked out of the cafeteria together. "Until then?" She smiled her goodbye at him and walked down the hallway toward her apartment. Billy let her go, not wanting to freak her out. His apartment was diagonal from hers. He'd been diligent about avoiding her, so he was pretty sure she didn't know.

He tapped the door frame and did an about-face. He'd grab a movie from the library and put it on for background noise while he journaled what happened tonight and how he felt about it. He hated doing the emotion thing, but he admitted writing the shit down helped him search out his thoughts and dig deeper than he was typically comfortable digging. Doc Wheeler and his damn homework. Billy shrugged his shoulders as he walked. He felt lighter and more settled than he had in ages. So, maybe Doc Wheeler knew what the hell he was doing.

"Hey, Billy, got a minute?" Mike White Cloud said as he entered the common room of the underground facility.

"Sure, what's up?" He liked Mike. The guy was no bullshit and ran the facility.

"A couple of things. Do you have any classes I'm not aware of scheduled on Saturday?"

"No, not really. No urgent missions are coming up, so we're doing firing range maintenance and working on class content."

"Would you go to Rapid and pick up a Guardian from the airport? It was easier to fit him into commercial air travel than wait for private transportation, and he arrives about five in the afternoon."

"Sure, are you building up?" The facility ebbed and flowed depending on what was happening. The Guardians that flowed through were normally housed above. It took a very high clearance to be invited downstairs, so Lillian had to have at least a Top Secret like him.

Mike nodded. "We are. He'll be working as an overwatch, which is the other thing I need to talk to you about. Alpha tried to contact you, but you weren't in your quarters or on your cell, so I figured you were bouncing around in the common areas."

That meant he had an assignment. Alpha only

called when he was in the bucket to deploy. "What's the job?"

"He's putting you on a Mercy Team as overwatch for the mission we're scaling up to cover."

The frown that creased his brow was instant. "Since when do Mercy Teams need an overwatch?" Mercy Teams were docs like Lillian that came in *after* a mission was over and the area was secure. They provided immediate help for teams and solo players, but one of the ground rules for using Mercy Teams was that their safety was to be ensured. Most doctors didn't carry weapons. There were a few exceptions, but they were rare.

"That's going to take a hot minute to brief you on. I'll brief you all once everybody arrives, but suffice it to say, the operation is high-visibility and high-value. The teams could be targeted to stop them from dispersing remedies to an emergent situation." Mike leveled him with a stare.

Billy worked through that line of reasoning. His shoulders slumped. Mike could only be talking about a handful of things. "Chemical or biological?"

"Unknown, and right now, that's the problem." Mike put his hands on his hips. "You'll be assigned to a team, but I'm not sure which one. Bosses want the overwatches to spend some quality time in long-distance target acquisition."

"What the hell are you anticipating, Mike?" Billy had worked as an overwatch for hundreds of missions. They never once worried about close-in threats or protection equipment.

"Everything and anything. So should you. This conversation is between us until all parties, including the Mercy Teams, are briefed, and that could be up to two weeks. I'll get you the flight details of the pick-up down in Rapid. Alpha wants a call in the morning."

Billy nodded and watched the man exit the common room. He glanced at the movies and shook his head. To hell with it. He would return to his apartment and hunker down. Sounded like he and a bunch of other players would be in for one hell of a ride. Billy frowned. That ride … his eyes darted after Mike. Those medics weren't prepared for it, and that could be a problem.

CHAPTER 7

Jacob King waited in the conference room for his brother Jason to arrive. He studied the area they'd need to protect in France. Guardian was assuming the inner cordon of security. The French police and military had been tasked to secure the outer cordon. Each delegation would have its own security, which was a nightmare of biblical proportions. He and Tori had assembled a team to coordinate arrival times and routes of travel to and from the venue. He had three response teams that would form the inner cordon. Charlie, Delta, and Echo teams specialized in Urban Warfare.

Jason walked in and leaned over the map with him. "What do you need?"

"The politicians to take this seriously." Jacob glanced at his brother.

"They are, but they won't cancel the meeting. Right now, it's assumed the intel we've received is being put out by parties that want to stop the signing of those documents. A lot of people will benefit if the war continues. Getting these parties to the table is of utmost importance. POTUS reminded me of that a few minutes ago. So, I ask again. What do you need?"

"A mock venue." Jacob stared back down at the map. "We need to know the routes of travel. Know the locations, see the room sizes, the exits, and entries."

Jason nodded. "So, nothing fancy, just fabricated boxes positioned correctly?"

"Something like that. Is Scott still at the ranch?"

"Yeah, he is." Jason straightened up and leaned on his cane. "I'll call Frank and see if we can use some land."

"Get Scott and his construction crew on this. The main building will need to be exact with door and window openings, but the others need to be a frame and covering. They don't have to be enclosed in wood. Canvas, vinyl, it doesn't matter."

"How long does he have to get this set up?"

"Two months? I want the teams to have time to run the scenarios, and then we'll deploy early, so everyone gets a walkthrough of the area before the principals arrive. We want to be in and out. I don't want any Guardian on the ground longer than necessary."

"I'll get this to Frank and Scott today." Jason nodded and pulled out a chair. He sat down with a sigh. "The latest intel hasn't changed. That concerns me."

"Me, too, but Adam and Mike forwarded the work that Dr. Montrose has been doing. She's good. She's given us options and narrowed the necessities based on similar compounds that might not be one hundred percent but would slow or diminish physical damages until the right compound is acquired. We can stage these things near the venue but not have them on hand. The French hospital system would need to be prepared for the influx of patients should this situation come to fruition."

Jason leaned forward to look at the papers Jacob slid in his direction. Jacob watched as his brother read the information. "She suggested the French government conduct mass casualty exercises based on gas and ingestible contaminates prior to the summit. I'll relay this to the POTUS's people and let them coordinate with the French."

"Good call." Jacob sat down and faced his brother. "I'm ready to go with the teams. Mike has three of the overwatches at the annex already. The last one to show up will be there on Saturday. He'll do the briefing then. But we have another suggestion for the Mercy Teams. It comes from Billy Pearson through Chief."

"What's that?"

"The Mercy Teams are not usually in the line of fire. They come in after the event. With them pre-positioned, Billy wants to give them training on what to do during certain situations. When the shooting starts, they should know what to do. How to handle a threat. What actions to take to mitigate a danger. He has a list of events and situations he wants to put the Mercy Teams through, so they aren't going in blind."

"Damn good idea, as long as they aren't pulled away from the medical training they'll need to go through in regard to this threat."

"I'll tell Mike it's a go under that condition," Jacob said. "This is a weird one, Jace."

"God, isn't that the truth?" Jason shook his

head. “I feel like a puppet with an unknown puppet master.”

Jacob got it. “I have to tell you, it’s almost like Guardian is being pulled into this. Did POTUS volunteer us?”

“I didn’t ask.” Jace sighed and took off his glasses. “So, it isn’t just me seeing this.”

“No. Tori, Joseph, and I have been talking. Normally, we’re behind the scenes. With this, we’re right out in the open. Well, at least as close to open as we’ve ever operated. The French have the resources to handle this. Why us? Who requested us?”

As Jason nodded, Jacob could see the worry on his brother’s face. “All good questions. As far as I know, it was the president himself. But … I’ll do some checking and ask Gabriel to do the same. I don’t like it, and I want us to proceed cautiously. Our priority is stopping whatever is planned.”

“At what cost?” Jacob shook his head. “We’ll be prepared for outside threats and possibly inside ones.”

Jason frowned. “Inside?”

“Tori said something to me this morning when we were going over the maps. She asked who has the most to gain if we fuck up and shit goes sideways? Especially if the president requested us to contain and prevent the situation."

Jason frowned. "No one. Well, except for those factions who don't want the peace treaty signed."

"You're not thinking devious enough, Jace. It's an election year next year."

Jason closed his eyes. "It would be egg on the president's face."

"That's one possibility. Then there are always those who are threatened by us."

"The Fates are a thing of the past. We've got a noose around Stratus's throat, and we're choking them out."

Jacob nodded and leaned back in his chair. "Yeah, we're winning on that front, but what about the unknown people who were working with Jonas? I'm still waiting for the next punch from that vector. Then, we have the remnants of the Rostova Group. Oscar Team is reporting a massive influx of money and organization based on the intel they've been getting in Mongolia."

Jace nodded. "All true."

"Do we have feet on the ground in these intel areas?"

"Us? No. The CIA and foreign intelligence agencies, yes." Jason leaned forward. "But that's about to change." He leaned on his cane and stood up. "We've got the baby class. It's time they go to work. No one knows them. They aren't on anyone's radar."

"Are they ready?"

"Is anyone really ever ready for this shit?" Jason asked. He pointed down at the medical brief Dr. Montrose completed. "The only thing she hasn't accounted for is radiological material."

"Which the French government has been tasked with scanning for starting a week prior to our arrival."

"Then we go in prepared. I want our people to check the area with our equipment when we land."

"My thoughts exactly." Jacob nodded. "No stone left unturned."

"Whatever it takes, brother."

"For as long as it takes," Jacob said and went back to studying the maps of the venue. The indoor locations were defensible. The grounds surrounding the conference. It was a fucking jigsaw of pathways, roads, trails, buildings, and landscaping that could hide a hundred people. And it would only take one …

CHAPTER 8

Billy sat across from Mike, Anubis, Asp, Alex, and Double D. He clarified, "So, it's a go?"

"As long as the medics aren't pulled from their required prep and training, yes." Mike nodded.

"Perfect. I'll work with Lillian on that, but this is my vision. Morning physical fitness training. We can't have them in the middle of this mess and expect them to perform like we do without conditioning them."

"Perform like we do?" Dixon cocked his head. "Dude, we have just over two months. If they're out of shape …"

"No, the medics are required to test annually and have a minimum standard they have to maintain." Mike pulled out a sheet of paper and passed it to Dixon, who shared the information with Drake.

"This isn't much better than out of shape." Drake pointed to the paper.

"But it's a starting point," Billy said. "I want them to be able to save themselves, no one else. These classes will be for their benefit."

"What kind of classes?" Anubis asked.

"Well, for one, what do they do if someone grabs them from behind?"

"So, close in defense?" Anubis nodded. "Joy has proven very efficient at teaching those techniques. She isn't in the bucket right now, so I'll see if she'd be willing to help."

"Good. How many of these medics can handle a handgun?" Billy asked Mike.

"Some won't touch them." Mike shook his head. "It's against the oath they took to do no harm."

"That's the doctors. What about the second team member? It could mean the difference between walking away and being toted out in a body bag." Billy pointed at the firing schedule he'd drawn up. "We need those who are willing to carry a weapon be familiarized with them and have time on the range."

"I second that. What else?" Asp asked.

"Scenarios. We have a mock venue being built. A 'What to do if …' type of thing. Where do you shelter if there's gunfire? This is an assumption, but each of the teams should have an assigned area. They'll need to know that place like the back of their hand. The mock venue will give them the spatial reference that could save their life."

"Are each of the team's overwatches snipers?" Alex asked.

"Yeah, about that." Mike cleared his throat. "Have you ever considered taking Kayla to Paris?"

Alex's eyes damn near bugged out. "Me? Dude, my leg is held together by bailing twine and super glue."

Mike chuckled. "I think that's a bit of an exaggeration, but yes, we need one more. We have Asp, Billy, and Specter available. We need the fourth team overwatch."

"Lyric is coming with me to Paris. Bring Kayla. Zero dark thirty on the day of the summit, we'll head to the venue. We'll be set up in overwatch positions well in advance. You won't need to run or climb anything. Lyric knows what I do." Asp shrugged. "She'll cover for us and keep Kayla busy. We'll say we're going on a men's day trip to

Normandy Beach or something and let them go shopping."

Alex dropped his eyes before he nodded. "Yeah, okay. But … I need to talk with Phil. Not specifics, but I need to make sure my being gone won't be a problem. The garage is my priority. My family is my priority."

"We get that," Anubis said. "Check today and get back to us. Otherwise, we'll need to figure out a workaround."

Alex nodded. "Will do."

"I'll let Lillian know what we're proposing." Billy shook his head. "I'm going to need help on this. Think of situations you've seen while working. What you'd wished someone did or didn't do during an operation. I know we can't plan for every eventuality, but we can give them some solid guidelines."

"Duck would work," Dixon said.

"Squat," Drake added.

"Cringe?" Dixon asked.

"What about cower or zigzag?" Drake laughed.

"That won't work if you have a sniper as an overwatch," Billy corrected the twins as he, Asp, and Alex all leaned back in their chairs and crossed their arms.

"That's a way to get your head blown off." Asp nodded.

Alex shook his head. "Movement is not our friend."

"Rut-roh, we pissed off the guys who shoot straight." Dixon elbowed Mike.

"Pay no attention to these two. They're noisy but harmless and will do their parts for physical conditioning. For the scenarios, the three of you and I will work together with Anubis. We'll meet here tomorrow after dinner. Billy will be back from Rapid, and you'll be done for the day at the garage, right?"

"Yep." Alex nodded. "If it's a go for Paris, I'll bring Kayla out, so she and Lyric can start planning."

"Perfect. Let me know, so I can fill her in on the trip and timeframe. She never asks for mission details, and I don't provide them," Asp said.

"I'll go down the hall and talk to Lillian about this."

"She's not there," Mike said as Billy started to rise. "She's in my office using Guardian's computer system to do some research."

"All right. *I'll* tell her tomorrow. We're going to

Hollister for lunch at the diner, and I can use the ride into town to explain it."

Mike shrugged and stood up. "As long as she gets briefed so she can build it into her training schedule."

"No worries."

"Hey, you're going to Rapid on Saturday, right?" Asp asked Billy as people started to drift out of the room.

Billy nodded. "Yeah. What's up?"

"Can you pick up Lyric's birthday present? I ordered and paid for it already, but with the build-up, I'm not sure I'll be able to make it down before her birthday."

"Sure. Just let me know what store."

"I'll send you a text and a picture of the receipt in case there are any issues. Also, I'm throwing a birthday party for her. Or she's throwing it for herself. She took over the menu and decorations. I'd like one thing to be a surprise."

Billy laughed. "Dude, she's a keeper."

"Don't I know it?" Asp clasped him on the shoulder. "See you later."

BILLY KNOCKED on Lillian's door and waited for her to answer it. He turned at the sound of someone running down the hall. "I'm here." Lillian was carrying her ever-present legal pads as she hustled to her apartment. "Sorry, I got involved in a video discussion with a couple of CBRN medical specialists."

"Calling in the big guns?" Chemical, biological, radiological, and nuclear defense, or CBRN, was one hell of a topic.

"Yes and no." She opened her door and invited him in. "I just want to change. I won't be a minute." She jogged back to the bedroom area. "Mike says you want to talk to me about training?" She called from the bedroom.

"Yeah. We can talk on the way to Hollister. What were you talking with the CBRN people about?"

"Crossovers in medical protocols and how to mitigate redundancy. I need to streamline the medications and the assessment protocols to speed the delivery of care." She came out of the bedroom carrying a pair of boots. The sight of her in skin-tight jeans and a white sweater that clung to her curves stirred something inside him he hadn't felt in a long time. She stopped and looked down at what she was wearing. "What? Is this okay? Do I need to change?"

"No, you look … damn, you look fine, Doc." He felt the air between them charge with a high-powered zing. Billy chuckled and rubbed the back of his neck. "And hopefully, that comment didn't make this lunch awkward."

She smiled at him. "Thank you, and no. We're going as friends, remember?"

"I do." But at that moment, he wished friendship wasn't a boundary. "Are you hungry?"

"Am I." She slipped on a boot. "I didn't get breakfast this morning because I overslept and forgot to eat last night."

"Forgot to eat? How is that possible?" Billy opened the door when she stood and grabbed her purse and coat from the kitchen stool they sat on.

"Sometimes I get so involved with my work I push away the annoyance of hunger pangs." She walked past him, and a hint of some floral scent trailed after her. The fragrance was the same she wore the night she'd stitched him up. It would forever be encased in his memory.

"So, tell me about this training. How long will it take? How many days? What are the parameters?" Lillian asked when they reached the end of the hall. He pushed the button that called the elevator down to them.

"Daily physical conditioning. The Mercy Teams have never been in the hot zone when you respond. You'll need to be able to save yourselves if shit goes sideways."

Lillian stepped into the elevator and turned to him. Leveling her gaze at him, she stated, "We save others when shit goes sideways."

"True, but you can't save them if you can't save yourself first, true?"

The door opened, and she stepped out, sliding the storage unit out of the way. "That's a valid point."

"Thank you." Billy's chuckle was fleeting because there wasn't anything funny about the Mercy Teams being in harm's way.

"That isn't so bad. We can allot time for that at the beginning of the day." They walked down the hall and out of the clinic. It was a warm March day, but they both needed coats. Warm in South Dakota was a measure of a couple of degrees, not a heat wave.

Billy opened the door of his truck for her, then went around to the driver's side. "Then, there will be situational scenarios and familiarization events we'll need to conduct."

She turned to look at him. "Why?"

Billy drummed his thumb on the steering wheel as he weighed the gravity of his next words. "This situation is unlike anything Guardian has done before. All our people are, to some degree, exposed and responsible for immediate responses. Have you ever been involved in a shooting or an explosion?"

She blinked at him and shook her head. "No."

"Would you know what to do if someone tried to attack you?"

"No." That was a quiet and truthful admission that laid bare the reality of their conversation.

"Those are the types of things we want to give you and your medical teams the basic understanding to deal with. That and firearms training."

Lillian's eyes popped wide, and she swung toward him with her mouth open. She held up a finger. Billy lifted a hand and interrupted whatever she was going to say. "To the ones who haven't taken an oath to do no harm or those willing to familiarize themselves to protect others."

"Oh." She visibly deflated. He guessed the response was from relief or resignation. After a moment, she nodded. "We'll need to look at the schedule I've built. There's wiggle room. I was going to give them downtime to decompress and go over the materials I'll be presenting."

"I'm sure we'll be able to work it. Just let me know when you want to get together."

"How about when we get back?" Lillian asked.

"Sounds like a plan," he eagerly agreed. The prospect of spending more time with her was something he looked forward to, probably more than he should. He gave a mental shrug. Fuck it. He wanted what he wanted.

"Now, I believe you were going to regale me with stories of two lifetimes spent with Isaac."

Billy laughed and shook his head. "You really do have a fantastic memory, don't you?"

"Pretty good," she admitted. "Helps in my line of work."

"Well, he and I were paired up in the military. We worked together as a team. Sniper and spotter. Fortunately, we were both damn good with the weapon, so we didn't have a designated spotter or sniper position. It's rare that happens."

"And you teach for Guardian?"

"We both do. I do deploy when an overwatch is needed, which happens to be with you and the others on this mission. Each of the medical teams will have a sniper overwatch."

Lillian stared out the window. It was a good five minutes before she spoke again. "Do you think it'll be that dangerous for us?"

"I hope not, but we're not going to sugarcoat anything at this point." Billy glanced over at her. "We'll be there along with three teams."

She seemed to digest his words for a moment. "But the team's primary concern will be to stop anything from happening to the people at the summit, right?"

"That's why you'll have a sniper assigned to your team. We'll be watching you. If anything goes wrong, we'll be able to provide cover, so you can get out of harm's way." Billy pulled onto the highway. "That's the reason for the training and scenarios we want to put your people through. Your safety."

"Then you should probably attend our classes, too."

"What do you mean?" Billy looked at her.

"Protective gear. If something is released, you won't do much good for us if you're dead."

"Oh, believe me, we know how to wear PPE,

but you're right. We should have an idea of what we're looking at, medically."

"And what to do if exposed," Lillian said absently.

"Right. But how about we think about other things for a while."

She turned to him and blinked. "Like what?"

"Like … how did you get started working for Guardian?" He chuckled. "Nothing classified, of course."

"Of course. Well, let's see. How far in the weeds do you want to go?"

"We have a good ten minutes to town, so maybe grasshopper level, not ant?" Billy laughed when she did.

"All right, grasshopper level. I worked in a lab—"

"Wait, I thought you were a medical doctor?"

She rolled her eyes. "I am. I did my internal medicine residency, then a fellowship in infectious disease. From there, I applied to positions at labs that studied those types of cases. I found one in Washington State in Spokane."

"So, Guardian recruited you from the lab?" Billy was trying to get his brain around that idea.

"No. Abe and I, he's my teammate on our

Mercy Team, worked with several others on a slate of programs. One of them, Dr. Dion Francis, and I had a relationship." She turned her head and stared out of the passenger side window.

Billy finally found something that made sense to him. "Ah, the narcissistic bastard."

"I didn't know it at the time." She shrugged. "He was the king of gaslighting."

"Gaslighting?" He'd heard the term before.

"Yeah. He had a way of making me doubt my judgment, even my memories. It was brutal."

"Psychological abuse."

"Yes. It took a couple of years of therapy to get over, and I won't let that happen again."

"Damn good on you. You got out, you got help, and you're on your own two feet. I'd say that was a win."

"Costly." She nodded. "But a win, nonetheless. Anyway, Dion was doing some morally ambiguous work at the lab, and I found out about it. I took it to our managers, who reported it to the administrators. Of course, he denied all of it and tried to cover it up."

"They didn't believe him, did they?"

"Not after we produced documents proving he was lying and doing what I accused him of."

Billy frowned. The bastard. What a dick. "What was he doing? In the lab, I mean."

"I think *that* might be classified. Suffice it to say, every ethical lab in the world had regulations prohibiting it."

"What happened to him?"

"Well, after he was fired, his medical license was suspended, and he was told he was being brought up on charges with the state medical board, he cleared out my bank account and disappeared."

"You don't know where he went?"

"Abe's brother Cash is the team lead for Foxtrot Team. He said he popped up in Europe." She reached out and put her hand on his arm. "Please don't get him in trouble for telling me. I was worried he'd show up again."

Billy covered her hand with his. "I don't think Cash would get in trouble for that, but don't worry, I won't say a word." Because he'd like to fly to Europe and punch that bastard in the face—just on general principle.

"Thank you. Anyway, I continued to work at the lab with Abe, but things were different. We were assigned cases that … Well, they were keep-busy type jobs, you know? I have my MD to fall back on, and Abe has a ton of certifications, paramedic, and such. One night, we were having dinner with Cash, and he suggested we consider working for Guardian. I called the number he provided the next day. Then I interviewed. That was fun."

"Why's that?"

"Well, after they finished their interview, I maybe drilled the doctor who was doing my intake."

Billy gave her a quick look. "Drilled?"

"You know, bored down to the bedrock. I wanted to know about Guardian. Who was the regulatory faction, and what type of restrictions would I be working under? Who would be my boss, where would I work, and what type of cases would I see? Anything and everything I could ask. The doctor, Maliki Blue, was a champ. He answered all my questions because I had my top-secret clearance from working at the lab." She chuckled. "That was the selling point. There was no hedging, no bull, just answers, and those he didn't know, he wrote down and found out for me. I liked the integrity of that interview. I was sold. Then I started meeting the people I'd be working with. I can't tell you how rewarding being on a

Mercy Team is. I travel, and I take care of the best people in the world."

"Guardian has always had a stellar reputation." Billy nodded. "I'm proud to be a member."

"When and how did you join? Nothing classified, of course." She winked at him.

"Right. Well, I was in Colombia working for another organization. Asp … ah, Isaac was there, too. Turns out the organization I worked for wasn't what they represented themselves to be. Guardian pulled me from that pile of shit and gave me the opportunity to work for them. I can't go into any detail, but Isaac and Guardian saved my ass. I'll always be loyal to them." He and the others who'd thought they worked for the company would have been killed during that raid if Isaac hadn't taken a chance on him and the friendship they'd formed in the military. He'd made mistakes and owned them. He glanced at her. "Did you find it hard to transition?"

"From the lab?"

"Yes, and taking care of people who are involved in covert operations?"

"Yes and no." She tipped her head, thinking through her answer. "I had to do a lot of questioning and research. I told you I asked a million questions. That was to belay my fear of being taken advantage of again. I also pick up shifts at an emergency room in Seattle when I can to get experience with the various types of wounds I see. Bullet wounds, stabbing, fights, fractures, and such. I realize Guardian personnel are the guys behind the badge, not the ones on the other side, so that alone put aside so many of my concerns. Covert or not, I'm helping the good guys, and that's critical for me."

"It should be critical for everyone," Billy agreed as he signaled for his turn into Hollister. "Welcome to the bustling metropolis of Hollister. I'll give you the nickel tour. Up here and to the left is the Bit and Spur. That's the local bar, but behind it, the owner, Declan Howard, has built a community hall where they hold dances and other events. A separate entrance from the bar so the ladies aren't offended by entering through the bar."

She turned to him and blinked. "You're joking?"

"No, ma'am. Things are still pretty old-fashioned around here." He turned down Hollister's main drag and pointed out things as he drove. "That's the hardware store. Gen's Diner is there, and behind it in the summer is one of the biggest gardens in the world. She uses the stuff out of the garden in her food, which keeps the prices way down. That's Phil Granger and Alex Thompson's garage. Phil is Alex's wife Kayla's uncle. Down here is a new building. One side is a bakery, which sells great breads and cakes. Next door is Kayla's shop. She has some basic clothes on hand but is also a tailor and quiltmaker. Down here at the end of the street are some small cabins where we house some Guardians who live here for an extended period." He did a U-turn and drove back. "That's the medical clinic, and on the back side are Dr. Wheeler's offices. He's the guy who helped me get my head straight about Mandy looking like you. Next is the post office. It's open about an hour a day as they sort mail, but there's a drop box there for outgoing mail. Then, the small grocery store with basics. They have the best meat. Mr. and Mrs. Sanderson own it, and they cut their meat to order. If you go down that road, you'll find the meat processing plant, and farther down is the stockyards."

He stopped, then pointed in the other direction. "That way is the school. All grades are housed in that one building."

"This is quite the little hamlet, isn't it?" She turned and looked in the direction of the school.

"When I first got here, I thought it was a joke. I mean, who would want to live out in the middle of nowhere, right? Turns out it was me. I'd want to live here. The people are completely genuine and not a bad apple in the lot." He did another U-turn and drove to the diner. "Now, to experience lunch with the locals. I advise you to pay close attention. There will be a quiz later."

Lillian laughed. "What happens if I don't pass?"

"Remedial eating, of course," Billy said as they got out of the truck. He opened the diner door for her, and the most amazing aroma met them. Lillian took a big breath and looked up at him. "I'm not sure that's a punishment."

Billy waggled his eyebrows at her. "Believe me, it isn't."

"Hey, look what the cat dragged in," a man said.

Billy walked over and extended his hand to Alex Thompson. "Dude, I keep telling you I turn up like a bad penny. I'd like to introduce you to Lillian Montrose."

Alex stood up. "Ma'am, a pleasure. This is my wife, Kayla." The women said hi to each other. "We'd ask you to join us, but we were just on our way out. I need to talk to Phil about a few things," Alex said.

"Don't let us stop you. We're going to get some food, then head back out to the ranch."

"It was nice meeting you," Kayla said as Alex helped her out of the booth.

"A pleasure," Lillian said, and the smile was real. He liked that about her. She wasn't standoffish.

"Hey, Billy," Ciera greeted as she passed by, "give me a second, and I'll bring out your lunch. What do you want to drink?"

"Hey, Ciera. I'll have a Coke. Lillian will have water," Billy said as they sat down in the next booth over from the one Alex and Kayla vacated.

"How did you know I wanted water?"

Billy snapped his head in her direction. "Oh, shit. I'm sorry. I just assumed. You chose water at the cafeteria. I can get you something else."

Lillian put her hand on his arm, stopping him from standing up. "No, water is fine. I would just prefer to have the say in what I order." She smiled at him. "That's a holdover from what we talked about on the way in."

Billy cringed. "Yeah, about that. We don't get to say what we want for lunch. They only serve one thing each day."

Lillian blinked. "Well, as long as I'm not the only one surprised."

"Here you go." Ciera put a glass of ice water and a soda on the table. "We're serving beef short ribs, mashed potatoes, gravy, candied carrots, and a side of bread and butter."

"Sounds fabulous," Lillian said.

Ciera smiled. "Thank you." She wiped her hand on her jeans, then extended her hand. "Hey, I'm Ciera. My husband Scott works out at the Marshalls' with Billy."

"Oh. It's so nice to meet you." Lillian shook Ciera's hand.

Ciera glanced up. "Well, drat, there goes the peace and quiet. Incoming, Billy." Ciera headed to the booth next to them to clean up the dishes.

"Incoming?" Lillian whispered. He smiled at the conspiratorial whisper.

Billy strained to see what Ciera was talking about, then laughed. "Ah, the town busybodies are en route. The one leading is Edna Michaelson. I think the others are Belinda and Doris or something like that. Edna believes in UFOs and Bigfoot. She's not complete upstairs, if you get my drift."

Lillian blinked at him and turned to the door as it opened. Edna walked in, smiled at him, then headed straight to their booth. "Mr. Pearson, how have you been?"

"Billy, ma'am, and I've been well. How have you and these lovely ladies been?" Billy gave her his best smile. He loved flirting with the older women, and he doubted many people took the time to actually visit with them. They seemed to preen under his attention.

CHAPTER 9

Lillian watched Billy turn on the charm. That smile and his full attention poured out on those elderly ladies was devastatingly effective. The two behind Edna sighed quietly and turned a pretty shade of pink. Edna put her hand on Billy's shoulder. "You are evil, young man. Who's your friend?"

"I'm not evil; I'm giving this county's beauties their due." Billy put his hand over Edna's, and the woman turned a brighter shade of pink. Billy turned to her. "This is a work colleague of mine, Lillian Montrose."

"Lillian, do you put up with this type of flattery when you're working with him?" Edna tittered a laugh that was so genuine Lillian had to smile.

"Actually, ma'am, I think he saves all the flattery for you and your friends."

Edna fanned her face. "Then he's wasting it." She pointed to the corner booth. "Ladies, we have work to do." The other two peeled off and headed over to the booth.

"Whatcha working on, Edna?" Billy asked.

"Well, it seems someone in Colorado submitted a video of Bigfoot. We've got maps, and we're trying to see if the one that was *reportedly* seen around here could get there without being seen."

"Bigfoot, huh?"

"Yes. Have you seen the video?" She pulled out her phone and swiped at the face. "Here." She leaned in and watched it at the same time as Billy. Billy's eyebrows rose. "That's a pretty clear video."

"And it's exactly like the one that ..." Edna glanced nervously at her. She shot a glance at Billy, then back at Edna.

"She's cool, Edna. She works with me."

"It looks exactly like the picture I took." Edna stood up straight. "Except the photo and the negative went missing."

"It did?" Billy's aghast question was just that side of being over the top.

"Yes. But I know what I saw, and plenty of

others saw that picture, too." She turned to the corner booth. "Right, ladies?"

"Definitely," one said, and the other just nodded shyly.

"Well, if you can track that monster, it would be a coup, for sure," Billy said. "Good luck with it."

"Thank you. Lillian, it was good to meet you."

"And you," Lillian blurted out, but it was more confusing than good. She waited until the lady sat down before leaning forward. "She really does think Bigfoot is a thing, doesn't she?"

Billy nodded. "And UFOs. Swears she's seen them. You can't make this stuff up. But she's a good old bird, and so are the others."

The bell on the door rang, and Lillian looked in that direction. A tall man wearing a sheriff's uniform walked in and took off his cowboy hat. Billy raised a hand. "Ken."

The man nodded and glanced at the women in the booth at the corner before coming over to shake Billy's hand.

"This is my friend, Lillian Montrose," Billy introduced.

"Ma'am. A pleasure." The man dipped his head a bit.

"Thank you. Nice to meet you, too." Lillian smiled at the politeness of everyone in the town.

"How's things?" Billy asked.

"Oh, you know. The same major crimes as always," the sheriff said, rolling his shoulders.

"Someone in trouble?" Edna asked from her seat at the booth.

"Nah. No one is out and about, Edna. Ladies." The man nodded at the booth. He turned back to Billy and made an eye motion toward the corner booth.

Billy whispered, "Tracking her Bigfoot to Colorado."

The sheriff's eyes closed briefly. "Well, that's something."

"Would you like to sit with us, sheriff?" Lillian asked.

"Thank you, but no. My wife will meet me here shortly."

"I heard she was looking to open an office here," Billy said and then turned to her. "Ken's wife Samantha was the state trooper around here, but she's passed the bar and is practicing law now."

"Is there much call for that up here?" Lillian looked between the two men.

Ken shrugged. "Some. Mostly contract law for

the ranchers. She does family law, too, so adoptions, divorces, settling estates, and so on. We're building an office just past the clinic when the freeze is gone."

"Are you building it?" Billy asked.

"Me and a bunch of volunteers. Scott will help as he can, but he's got a big project he's just undertaken."

Billy nodded. "Let me know when it is, and I'll spread the word out at the ranch."

"That's mighty thoughtful. Thank you," Ken said, then turned as the door opened. A woman with dark red hair stepped through into the diner. She smiled, waved at the corner booth, and moved over to Ken, giving him a quick kiss. "Lillian Montrose, my wife, Samantha."

Lillian shook the woman's hand, and they said hi to each other just as Ciera came out of the kitchen, heading their way with a tray full of plates. "We'll let you eat," Ken said and directed his wife to another booth.

"All this?" Lillian said after the plates were put in front of them.

"Yes, ma'am. We've got some to-go containers if you can't finish it." Ciera chuckled. "But I've seen this one eat. He won't need them."

"Hey, I happen to resemble that remark," Billy said indignantly, which both she and Ciera laughed at before Ciera headed back to the kitchen.

"Oh, man," Lillian said as she tasted the potatoes and gravy. "This is so good."

"I've never had a bad meal here," Billy said as he buttered his dinner roll.

Lillian cut into her short rib. "This town is …"

"Crazy?" Billy supplied.

"No." She shook her head. "Charming." It reminded her of those old black-and-white shows where people would sit outside in the evenings on their porches and talk with people who strolled by.

"I like it. Didn't think I would, as I told you, but it just kind of … fits. Comfortable, you know?"

She nodded as she ate the fall-off-the-bone tender beef. "Everyone knows everyone."

"And they're all up in each other's business, too," Billy said but then stopped. "Until someone needs help. Then, everyone pulls in the same direction. The things this town is capable of doing are pretty amazing."

"I imagine they're pretty self-sufficient for the most part. They kind of have to be, don't they?" She glanced out the window. There wasn't much of anything close to them. "How far is the nearest town?"

"Of any size? That would be Belle Fourche, which is hours south of here. Rapid City is an hour or so past that. That's where I'm going tomorrow." Billy took a big bite of his beef after he spoke.

"What are you going to Rapid for?" She laughed when he stopped chewing. "I'll wait."

He nodded and wiped his lips before speaking. "I have to pick up one of the overwatches from the airport, and Isaac asked me to pick up a birthday present he'd bought for his wife while I was down there. Do you want to come?"

Lillian blinked at the question and put her fork down as she thought about it. Finally, she shook her head. "I'd like to, but I have too much to do. If we can get the schedule sorted tonight, I'll be back on track, though. Maybe the next time you go?"

"That sounds like a deal," Billy said. "So, tell me about you."

Lillian glanced up at him. "Like?"

"How did you decide to become a doctor? What do your parents think about it? Do you have any brothers or sisters? What's your favorite movie?" He shrugged. "Normal stuff."

She chuckled. "Well, I've always known I

wanted to be a doctor. My grandfather was a doctor, and he had a big impact on my growing up. My mom and dad are living the retired life in Florida and think I work for a medical transport company, which explains why I'm off on a moment's notice. I visit them a couple times a year and hear all kinds of complaints if I miss either Thanksgiving or Christmas." She laughed. "But I love to spend time with them, and I try my hardest to call every week or so. They have such an active social life I feel like I'm the old person in the family. What about your family?"

"Gone. Dad to cancer and Mom to grief shortly after that. They were soul mates. You know what I mean? They lived for each other. It was something I didn't understand until recently. Finding a love like that is something special."

"It is." She stared at him for a moment. "What's your favorite movie?"

"Wow. Of all times?" He leaned back and narrowed his eyes. "*Starship Troopers*."

She snorted and then choked on the bite of food she'd just taken. "You're joking, aren't you?"

"No way! One, it has NPH in it. That dude is legendary. Second, it has massive bugs that can read your mind. Third, space travel, laser weapons, and even a bit of romance for the women. Have you watched it?"

"I have." She tried to hold back her laughter.

"More than once?"

Man, she didn't want to admit it, but she nodded. "Five or six times."

Billy threw back his head and laughed, clapping his hands together. "I knew I liked you."

She pointed her fork at him. "It isn't my favorite, though."

"What is?" he asked as he took a bite of roast beef.

"*Iron Man* with RDJ."

"Why?"

"Because the movie is excellent. Tell me I'm wrong."

Billy smiled widely. "I'm Team Cap."

Lillian narrowed her eyes at him. "You're not a rule follower, are you?"

"Not usually." He gave her a cheeky grin.

"Figures." She felt the warmth of that smile to the tips of her toes. God, the man was so sexy; more than that, he was fun, engaging, and had a sense of humor she really enjoyed. They visited about other things as Lillian did a good amount of damage to the beef and ate all the carrots and potatoes. Leaning back against the booth, she patted her stomach. "I'm going to burst."

"Then you don't want your dessert?" Ciera said as she came in their direction with what looked like two pieces of pumpkin pie.

"To go, maybe?" Billy said as he patted his own stomach.

"I'll get these boxed up," Ciera said, doing an about-face and heading back into the kitchen.

"Was I right, or was I right?" Billy asked with a sexy half smile across his face.

Lillian instantly lowered her eyes at the thought. *Sexy?* Yes, *but no! No, this is a friendship. Pure and simple. Friends only. Friend zone. This line and no further!* Besides, she only had a short time there, and it was obvious Billy loved where he worked. She blew out a breath and nodded, checking her thoughts before looking up at him. "You were absolutely correct. Fantastic food. Thank you."

"Are you ready for that drink?"

Lillian groaned. "No, especially if we're revising those schedules this afternoon."

"Okay, raincheck on that." Billy pulled out his wallet and dropped cash onto the table. He didn't argue or press her for the drink, which she was grateful for. She liked talking with him because he was genuine, even if a bit mischievous. But that just added to his charm.

Lillian took his hand to exit the booth and reprimanded herself for thinking of him as charming. She needed to stop it. Just because he was handsome … *Dear heaven, she had to stop that.*

"Lillian?" Billy said.

"I'm sorry, what? I must have fallen into a food coma."

"I asked if you needed anything in town before we headed back." He waved to the sheriff and his wife and said goodbye to Edna before opening the door.

"Wait! I have your desserts," Ciera said as she jogged to the door with a small bag.

"Thank you," Lillian said, taking the bag from her.

"So, do you need anything?" Billy asked again.

"I need a walk," Lillian said as she wrapped her jacket around her.

"Then let's do it." Billy took the bag from her and put it on the hood of his truck.

"Won't someone take it?" She glanced at the food.

"Nope." He jumped back up onto the wooden

boardwalk and offered her his elbow. He asked in a pretty good British accent, "May I escort you on a parade around town?"

She hooked her hand through his arm and laughed. Mimicking his accent, she replied, "Please, sir. Once again, enlighten me with the highlights of this delightful town."

Lillian laughed as Billy doffed his hat to people they passed on the walk around the small town. She met the woman who ran the bakery because Billy wanted to stop in and buy some bread to support the store. They stopped at the small clinic, and Billy introduced her to Dr. Zeke Johnson and his wife, who ran the front of the office. They chatted a bit before parading down to the general store, where Billy bought five packs of cookies.

"Why so many?"

Billy frowned at her. "Oh, that's right, you've never seen Isaac eat, have you?"

"Ah … no." She glanced down at the chocolate and cream-centered cookies. "That's a lot of sugar."

"For most people," Billy agreed as he paid for them. "We stockpile them. Sometimes Lyric gets crazy and tries some pretty out-there food. She's a great cook, but once upon a time, she wasn't." Billy laughed. "Poor Isaac lost about twenty pounds before she was through that vegan phase."

"So, you're hoarding against the possibility of it happening again?" Lillian laughed as they walked out and crossed the street back to where the truck was parked.

"Exactly! See, you get it, right?" Billy's smile was a mile wide.

"Not at all." Lillian laughed and then laughed harder when Billy looked completely crestfallen at her words. She hadn't had so much fun in years. Billy opened her door for her and treated her like she was special. She sighed happily when he grabbed the slices of pie and added them to his purchases before getting into the truck.

As they pulled onto the highway, Lillian said, "Thank you for today. I didn't realize how much I needed it."

"The food was amazing, wasn't it?" Billy agreed.

"Not just the food. The laughter, mixing with other people, all of it. I don't get out much, mostly by choice. Today reminded me I need to make an effort to be more present in my own life."

"Whoa. That was kind of deep." Billy glanced at her. "I was going for fun."

Lillian laughed again. "Blame the deep part on therapy."

He snorted. "I will, but only if you blame anything deep I say on my therapist, too. I'm not that kind of guy. All shallow waters here, I'm afraid."

"You're exactly that kind of deep. I think you're pretty amazing, Mr. Pearson."

Billy looked over at her and smiled that sexy and mischievous half-smile. "Right back at you, Dr. Montrose."

Lillian felt her face heat and glanced out the window, taking in the winter-deadened landscape surrounding them. She barely saw it as feelings that had been buried forever crept toward the surface. She could really fall for that man if she weren't careful.

CHAPTER 10

Billy leaned against the wall at the Rapid City Regional Airport and watched the people funnel through the terminal toward the baggage claim. His pickup was easy to spot. He'd been given a full briefing on the guy. Lifting off the wall, he walked to the man. "Whatever it takes, my friend."

"As long as it takes." The man extended his hand. "I don't have any bags. I was told I'd be supplied with what I need."

"We've got you. Let's go. My name is Billy."

The man hesitated. "Ah …"

"Specter. Chief told me. You can go by your code name as long as you're at the ranch and the annex. Everyone does. I was never assigned one, hence the awkwardness just now." Billy laughed. "Besides, all the best code names are taken."

They walked out the doors into the cold air. "What do you do for Guardian?" Specter asked as they got into his truck.

"Today, I'm an errand boy. Yesterday, I was a tour guide. Tomorrow, I'll assess how well you shoot, and then I'll teach classes. So, I guess I'm a jack of all trades and master of none. Well, one. I can outshoot anyone."

Specter snorted. "Not likely."

Billy let out a hell of a laugh. "Oh, fuck, a challenge? Really, so soon, son? Have you no respect for your elders?"

"One, you're not old, definitely not old enough to call me son, and two, what shooter in their right mind doesn't think they can outshoot everyone else?"

Billy rocked his head back and forth. "I'm older than you think, but I'll give you point number two. It seems to be a personality trait for sure." Billy pulled onto the highway, heading back toward Rapid from the south. "Hungry? It's a serious drive back to the annex."

"I could eat. The last time I had real food was in

Sydney. I didn't have time to grab anything in Dallas."

"Dude, how are you upright? Fast food or a sit-down restaurant?"

"I'd kill for a double cheeseburger and a couple of orders of fries."

"Nope, we don't kill without authorization. But fast food it is." Billy headed to the first burger joint on the way north. He fed the assassin and then shut up. The guy was asleep within three miles of finishing his food. Billy got it. Air travel sucked, especially when you had to keep your guard up. Being somewhere where you could relax, well, it was a luxury.

Speaking of luxuries, he couldn't quite get his day with Lillian out of his mind. After they returned to the annex, they spent a couple of hours reviewing her schedule and what he thought they'd planned for training.

"Days off aren't going to happen, are they?" she asked when he pointed to the time she'd scheduled as off time on her templates. "But we're shoving a lot of information on them. They need time to understand it, to go over it."

"That's a luxury we don't have." Billy shook his head. "Every day should have something, either famil-

iarization training or your classes. They have to be prepared."

Lillian took a deep breath and released it slowly. "I really hope this is all for naught."

"There is a threat. The context is still broad, but Guardian will find out more. They're working on it, and if there's one thing I know beyond a shadow of a doubt, they'll give us as much information as possible."

"Can't they just move the date of the summit? I mean, do it tomorrow and take everyone by surprise."

"It took a year of work to get the parties to agree to this date. Changing it would only cost more lives. The cease-fire is tenuous as it is." Billy shook his head. "We prepare for the worst and hope for the best. Whatever it takes."

"For as long as it takes." She looked up at him. "We get to say it, too. We're family."

"You get to say it because you fix us up, and you're an important part of the team. Never forget that." He watched as her eyes scanned his expression as if to check to see if he were lying to her. Man, he'd love to sucker punch that fucking dick who treated her so badly. He smiled at her, and she lowered her eyes. The woman was afraid. Of him? Maybe. Maybe of men in general. He'd fix that ... He picked up his schedule and pretended to scan it. Why? Why did he want to fix it? Well, stupid,

because she's gorgeous, and now that you've unpacked your baggage and know she's nothing like Mandy, you can see yourself with this sexy woman, can't you?

Yeah, he could. And that was a problem, not for him, but for her. She wasn't the type of woman a man took to bed and then said, "Thanks, see you around" to. She was a woman he'd want to date for the long haul. He'd seen Asp and Lyric's relationship grow over the years. He wanted something like that. Something that was exciting but had a foundation built out of stone.

Billy sighed as he saw the turn to the ranch. He'd follow her lead but also let her know he wanted to see her again. He wasn't sure just how he would accomplish that little feat, but given time, he'd figure it out. He was a tenacious son of a bitch when he wanted something. He slowed to pull off the highway onto the ranch's access road, and Specter woke instantly. "We're about five minutes from the annex," Billy said in way of explanation.

"Damn." Specter rubbed his face. "Sorry about crashing."

Billy waved him off. "Never stay awake if you can sleep."

"That's the truth." Specter yawned. "Anubis said my weapon would be here?"

"It arrived this morning. I'll show you where she is, and you can put bullets down range tomorrow. As a matter of fact, we can have a little friendly competition between the four of us deploying, just to make it interesting."

Specter chuckled. "Why do I feel like I'm being set up?"

"What? No." Billy made an innocent expression. Specter's laughter was contagious.

When they stopped laughing, Specter asked, "Do you know the details of the mission?"

"I do. Each of us will provide overwatch for a medical team."

The man frowned. "Unusual."

"There's nothing about this mission that's usual. Take my word for it. But then again, it's unusual times in the world." Billy pulled up to the clinic. "Come with me." He waited to be buzzed in because it was after hours, then took Specter to the supply closet. The man's eyebrows rose as Billy moved the shelving unit and walked into the elevator. The doors closed, but the elevator didn't move. "You need to look into that camera." Billy pointed to the camera in the corner of the elevator.

Specter did as he was told. "Authenticate poltergeist." Mike's voice came over the speaker.

"Apparition," Specter replied.

The elevator engaged and started its downward trek. Specter frowned and turned to him. "Why did you wait until I was in the elevator before you challenged me with an authentication?"

Billy shrugged. "You hadn't seen anything that was classified to that point."

The door opened, and Specter blinked. "Holy shit."

"Welcome to the annex." Billy walked out of the elevator and headed down the hall. "Your rooms will be down this hall. This is mine. There's a vacant one on either side, so probably one of those." He motioned to the apartments. "Down here and to the right is the cantina, cafeteria, chow hall, call it what you want. They have a walk-in full of food for us." They continued to walk. "This is the great room."

"No shit." Specter looked up and did a three-sixty. "How in the hell did they build this?"

Billy glanced around. "Carefully, I assume."

"Smartass," Specter chuffed.

Billy turned to him. "You're just now figuring that out? Man, they're recruiting slow assassins these days, aren't they?"

Specter blinked, then belted out a laugh. "Fuck, man. You're crazy. You realize that, right?"

"He does," Asp said from the other side of the great room. "You're late." He walked toward them. "Asp."

"Ah, finally, a name I recognize." Specter extended his hand. "Specter."

"Good to meet you. Everyone's in the conference room. Let's go."

Billy let Asp take the lead and followed them to the conference room. The next couple of months would be one for the books. Hopefully, they'd get more intel and be able to zero in on a threat.

* * *

THEY'D ATTRACTED A CROWD. The bullets continued to go down range. The targets were moved farther and farther out. Anubis, Double D, Mike, Frank Marshall, and the ranch foreman, John, were quiet as they stood and took turns looking through a scope at the targets each of them obliterated.

Specter nodded toward Alex. "What happened?"

Alex was moving slowly in the cold, and his limp was obvious after getting into position so many times today. "Training accident. His leg is held together by nuts and bolts."

"And bailing wire," Alex said from the ground.

There was a rumble of laughter from the men standing behind them. Alex drew in a breath, released half of it, and a millisecond later, the rifle bucked against his shoulder.

Billy leaned down to look through his scope. "Dead center."

"Dead being the operative word." Alex rolled onto his back and accepted Asp's offer of an assist. "If y'all want to continue this pissing contest, you can do it without me. My leg is killing me."

"I'm done," Asp said. "We've proven we're good."

"You have." Specter laughed. "For old guys." The man pointed at Billy. "His words, not mine."

"I *was not* speaking about them," Billy defended himself. "I was talking about myself."

"Right," Asp said. "Heads up." He nodded down the hill. Billy turned around and smiled. "Hey. What are you doing out here?"

"Well, I figured I'd see just how good you guys were with a gun," Lillian said as she approached. "I briefed my people this morning about the physical and familiarization training."

"How did that go?" Mike asked.

"Better than I thought it would. Minor grumbles about the time of morning for physical training, but everyone agreed the familiarization training was needed."

"A good idea," Frank Marshall said. He nodded his felt cowboy hat toward Lillian and greeted, "Ma'am." Then he and John headed back down the hill toward the ranch.

"Let me show you the target. Billy, you take the next shot." Asp called Lillian over to the scope. Billy took his weapon and positioned it on his marks. He relaxed and performed the motions he'd done a thousand times. He knew the wind hadn't changed. There wasn't even a breeze, which made the shots easier but no less technical. He lined up his sight picture and drew a breath, releasing about half of it. The barrel on the rifle rolled in a small figure-eight motion, which was stabilized by his tripod. He slowly squeezed the trigger of his rifle and watched as his bullet flew to its target. He put it directly in the center of the target's head. Was he showing off? Hell, yes, but he needed Lillian to see he was damn good, especially since they drew teams today. He'd drawn Lillian and Abe, Mercy Team Five. Of course, the fact he knew which folded sheet of paper had her team listed was irrelevant. He wouldn't let anyone else watch over her. It was his mission.

"Wow." He heard Lillian's exclamation before rising to his knees. "That was amazing."

Billy glanced over at Specter, who winked at him and said, "He's good for an old man."

Lillian barked out a laugh. "If he's old, what does that make me? Ancient?"

Specter blinked, and his mouth fell open. "That's not what I meant, ma'am."

The men who remained laughed as Specter sputtered. Billy slung his rifle and picked up his bucket of brass. "Alex and I were just going down the hill to clean our weapons. Want to come with us?"

"I'd love to. It's cold out here."

"That it is," Alex said, limping over to his brass bucket.

"Leave that. I've got it," Specter said. "You get out of the cold. We need you in France."

"Thanks, man," Alex said and limped toward Billy.

"You shouldn't walk all the way back to the clinic." Lillian was beside Alex. "What happened to your leg?"

"We aren't going to the clinic," Billy said and took Alex's weapon from him, slinging it on the same shoulder as his rifle. "Care for a crutch?"

"Thanks." Alex threw his arm around Billy's shoulder as they walked down the hill. "Follow us, Doc," Alex said.

Lillian was right beside the men. "Seriously, what happened?"

"Well, I was in a training accident and basically totaled my leg. The doctors bolted me together and discharged me. I'm usually not this gimpy, but I stayed out too long trying to outshoot these guys."

"The cold makes the muscles stiffen around the hardware?"

"Ma'am, just about everything does that. I've learned to live with the ache, but usually, I'm not being stupid about it either. I'll soak in a hot tub tonight and be right as rain tomorrow."

"Kayla's going to bust your ass for this." Billy laughed as they stopped in front of the small shed.

"Yeah, she will," Alex agreed.

"Lillian, could you get the door?" Billy nodded to the shed. She frowned but opened the door. Billy angled Alex through the door, and Alex hit the hidden switch to open the back of the shed and reveal the elevator.

"Well, dang it, I wish I knew about this sooner. My feet are freezing." Lillian laughed as they all piled into the elevator.

"Those are not cold weather boots," Billy agreed. The high-heeled boots were a brown leather but thin with fancy designs.

"But they *are* cute," Lillian said, lifting her foot. "And in my defense, I didn't know how far the firing range was from the clinic. Talk about a hike."

The elevator door opened, and the warm air flooded the elevator car. "Oh, man, I needed this," Alex grunted as he made his way down the hall by himself. "I now wish I'd never laughed at the old guys in the unit who said they could tell the weather was going to change by the ache in their knees."

"This is our area," Billy said as the automatic lights came on in the range's room.

"Wow." Lillian walked over to the weapons mounted in racks against the wall. "Do you shoot all these?"

Billy put their rifles on the cleaning table and moved a stool over for Alex to sit on. "Yeah, but these rifles are what we practice with the most."

"They're bigger than these." Lillian sat down on a stool, too. "Can I help?" She took off her gloves and looked at Billy expectantly.

Both he and Alex chuckled. "With any other weapon, I'd say yes." Billy broke down his rifle, as did Alex. "These are highly personalized, and we're kind of territorial about them. But we'd enjoy some conversation while you wait for us to finish."

Alex reached for the cleaning kit Billy had put on his side of the table. "It isn't anything against you personally."

"Oh, no, I understand. I wouldn't let either of you mess with my equipment, but I thought I'd offer." She laughed.

"Have you been to France before?" Alex asked her. "My wife isn't aware of the reason we're going, but it's her first time, and she's excited. She has a list of at least twenty things she wants to do and see."

"I went to Paris after I finished my fellowship. It was my treat to myself for finishing my final school. I scraped and saved to go because, believe me, a resident and then a fellow doesn't make good money. I went on a shoestring budget, but I was able to see the Louvre. I walked to the Eiffel Tower from my hotel and the Arc de Triomphe. There was a place, Painter's Square, I think it was called. Artists sitting outside painting. Little shops all around the place. It was wonderful. I ate at bistros and people-watched. It was a great week." She unbuttoned her coat. "Is this where you store your hoarded cookies?"

Billy laughed. "It is. That cabinet. Help yourself." He nodded toward it. She hopped off her stool and walked over to the cabinet.

"Oh, man, you weren't joking, were you?"

Billy glanced over as she looked at the filled cupboard. "If health nuts ever overrun us, the three of us would still manage to die of diabetes."

"I don't doubt it." She pulled down a foil-wrapped item from a white box. "I have a weakness for these."

"Who can resist chocolate cake, fluffy vanilla frosting all rolled up and covered with more chocolate?" He couldn't. They were his favorite, too.

"Meh, I prefer the ones with marshmallow and coconut," Alex said as he rammed a rod through the barrel of his rifle.

"Yeah, the pink ones," Billy taunted.

"Screw you, they're good." Alex tossed a cleaning brush at him.

Billy caught it and put it on the table. "It's okay. I'm sure your masculinity is not in question."

"Since when?" Asp asked as he and Specter walked into the armory area. "He eats pink food."

"Don't disrespect good food because of food coloring," Specter said as he walked over to the brass bucket.

"Red food coloring is bad for you," Lillian said just before biting into her chocolate cake.

"And all that sugar is healthy?" Alex asked.

"Absolutely." Lillian made nummy sounds that drew Billy's eyes to her face. The pure bliss as she ate her snack cake was evident, and damned if his cock didn't twitch with interest at the sounds she made. Dear God, she was the most amazing woman. He'd been such a fool to think she was anything like Mandy. He stared at her as she took another bite of the snack cake. Thank God he had, though; otherwise he'd never have made it to that point. He could see the cliff's edge, and he was running straight toward it. He had every intention of falling for Lillian and he wasn't going to slow down. Specter poured a can of brass into the brass barrel, which shifted his attention. He glanced over at Asp, who had a shit-eating grin on his face. *Bastard.* He glowered at his best friend, which only made the man's smile wider.

He finished cleaning his rifle as he listened to Lillian talk with the other men. Perhaps he went a little faster than he should have, but he'd return and ensure his weapon was perfectly clean later. He put his rifle on the rack. "Alex, can we help you back?" *Say no. Say no. Just fucking say no.*

"Nah, I'm good here. I'm going to finish up and head back with Asp and Specter."

"See ya." He extended his arm to Lillian. "Ma'am, may I play tour guide once again?"

She smiled widely and put her hand through the crook of his elbow. "Thank you, kind sir." They walked leisurely down the corridor that would eventually connect them with the rest of the annex. "You didn't mind me coming out to watch you today, did you?"

Billy whipped his head around to look at her. "Good God, why would I mind?"

Lillian looked down and shrugged. "Old fears, maybe."

Billy stopped and turned toward her. "I'm not him."

She looked at him and said clearly, "And I'm not her."

"Whoa." The truth hit hard, almost like a physical collision of her past and his. He leaned back against one of the supports of the corridor. "Those two sentences packed a lot of shit, didn't they?"

She nodded. She was tense, her lips in a tight line. "I'm not going to beat around the bush, Billy. I like you. You make me laugh, and I can talk to you. I like that. I think you're handsome, and I find you attractive. But I'm not ready for a relationship."

He crossed his arms over his chest and smiled at her. "Yeah, you think I'm attractive?"

She rolled her eyes and started walking. "That's what you pulled out of what I just said?"

He jogged to catch up with her and dropped his arm over her shoulders as they kept walking. "I think you're sexy as hell, Doc. I like spending time with you. There is this, I don't know, ease, I guess, between us, and that's something I think is hard to come by. I don't think you're Mandy. The differences are legion."

Lillian laughed and turned to him as they walked. "Legion? Who says that?"

"Really, that's what you pulled out of what I just said?" He parroted her earlier question.

She sighed. He could sense both frustration and amusement. "Can we keep this casual?"

"This?" Billy wanted clarification. *Casual sex? Casual touching? Casual dating?*

"What's happening here," she clarified, but not enough, in his opinion.

He drew a deep breath and jumped in with both boots still on. "Well, that depends on what you think casual is. If you're drawing a line, I need to know where it is, so I don't step over it. I mean, I'm never going to push you for more than you want to give. That will never happen, but you need to define the parameters for me."

They walked a bit farther, the lights in front of them illuminating and the lights behind them shutting off as they walked. "I've never had casual sex."

The word sex hung between them, and it was a super-charged word, wasn't it? Billy blinked and jerked his head in her direction. Sex. *Yep, that was at the heart of it, wasn't it?* "Because you're not wired that way or because you've never had the opportunity?"

"I don't know, both, maybe?" The words were colored with uncertainty and maybe a bit of vulnerability, which was completely unlike her. She sighed. "I've never had sex outside of a serious relationship."

"Well, by my definition, if you're having sex with someone, you're in a relationship. Just saying."

"And that's what worries me." She looked up at him. "What if this attraction doesn't work out?"

Billy stopped again and faced her. "What if it does?"

She crossed her arms and looked down. Her body language showed the conflict she was talking about. "Maybe that's what scares me most."

He tucked his finger under her chin and lifted her gaze to his. "Worrying about things that haven't happened is unproductive. How about we start with this." He lowered and touched his lips to hers. He felt her tremble under his kiss. The shiver spoke volumes. He licked her lips, and she let him in. She was so tentative; it gave him pause. He lifted away and studied her face. Her eyes were closed, and her lashes were dark against her fair skin. When she opened her eyes, he smiled at her. "Let's just take things a step at a time."

"Do I kiss like her?"

Her words wiped the smile off his face as if they were a bucket of ice water pulling him from the warmth of the moment. He narrowed his gaze.

"No." He brushed her hair back from her cheek. "Do I kiss like he did?"

She stared at him, then shook her head. "No. You don't. He still haunts me. Even after all the work and therapy. Does she still haunt you?"

"The guilt does. I'm learning how to manage that. What feelings did he leave you with?" He'd learned a lot from Dr. Wheeler but still had those feelings and probably always would.

"Fear. No—that's not the right word, but it's as close as I can get. Letting anyone have that much power over my life again. Maybe it is fear or perhaps extreme caution."

At her words, the lights in the tunnel went out. She gasped, and Billy raised his hand. The motion detection lighting turned back on. "You have nothing to fear from me." He drew her hand through his arm, and they started to stroll. "I looked up gaslighting. I couldn't imagine what that did to your confidence. The thought of what you went through makes me sick."

"I questioned my sanity at times. If it hadn't been for Abe … Well, things were bleak for a while." She drew a shaky breath. "Mental abuse is just as real as physical abuse."

"It is." He put his hand over hers. "I'll make you

a solemn promise. I'll never play games with you. I say what I mean, and I've never laid a hand on a woman in anger. I never will. My parents raised a gentleman."

She leaned her head against his arm as they walked. "Coming up to the range today took every ounce of courage I had. I turned back two or three times."

"Well, I'm glad you made it. Next time, though, you should wear snow boots." He aimed to change the tone and make things lighthearted. Her laugh was a delicious reward. "Do you have anything on your schedule tonight?"

She shook her head. "No. Tomorrow morning starts all the fun. The teams are above ground and getting themselves settled. I told them I was staying with a friend since Mike told me they couldn't know about the below-ground facilities because of their clearance level."

"Well, you're not technically telling a lie. You're staying across from me, and I'm a friend. Right?"

She turned to look at him. "Across from you?"

"Diagonal. To your right as you exit your door," he confirmed.

"And how did I not know this?"

"I may have made sure you didn't see me

coming and going while I was working on putting my head straight." Billy shrugged. "Sue me. I'd made a fool of myself enough."

"You *did* act weird." Lillian chuckled and turned to walk backward while looking at him. And did she look … her gaze went from top to bottom. And yep, his cock kicked to life again. The electricity between them sizzled so damn hot that if anyone walked between them, they'd be nuked.

"Hey, give me some credit. I still am weird, just not *that* kind of weird." Billy gave her a smile and lifted his eyebrows a couple of times. "Have dinner with me. Maybe as a little more than friends." *A lot more than friends, and who needs food?*

"I like your weirdness, just saying, and I thought you'd never ask." She licked her lips. "That snack cake won't hold me until morning." They stopped walking, and he heard her stomach growl. His mind flipped from sex to caretaker in less than a second.

He narrowed his eyes at her. "Don't tell me you forgot to eat today."

She made a face. "Guilty."

He didn't like that she didn't take care of herself. "What was so important you forgot to eat?"

"Well, greeting each of the teams as they came

in. Getting them settled and having our first meeting. Explaining our conditioning program and familiarization requirements. Going over the intel we had so far. That wasn't me. We had a video conference with Jacob King. Then, I had to bolster my courage enough to start the walk up to the range. Then actually *walking* up to the range."

She looked at him from under those long lashes. Damn, he had to struggle to keep focused on her needs and not his. But fuck his libido; she was more important. "Am I going to have to make sure you take care of yourself?" Billy tsked. "Don't answer that. From here on out, I'll be your appointed food monger. Three squares a day, ma'am. No less."

She laughed, and the sound vibrated through every nerve ending in his body. His arms tingled with gooseflesh. What she did to him was insane. "I think you'll be too busy to be my food monger."

"Nonsense," he dismissed her concern using every ounce of self-control he had. "It will be my privilege and honor. Starting now." He opened the door at the end of the corridor, and they stepped into the great room.

Lillian moved over the threshold and glanced

around. "Well, now, I know where I am. I wondered where this door led."

"And now, you know. There are several I don't have a clue about, but I figured if I needed to know, the powers that be would tell me."

"That's the truth." She chuckled as they walked toward the cafeteria.

Billy stopped her before they entered the dining area. "I'm glad you came up. I'm even happier you told me what you're feeling." The openness of their conversations was a new thing for him, and it only increased his desire for her.

She smiled up at him. "So am I."

CHAPTER 11

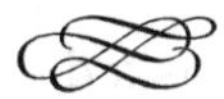

Joseph King waited for the rest of the team to join the video. He had an ugly gut feeling about the mission. He didn't like it. Not one iota.

When Jewell put Jason on the screen, Joseph didn't hesitate to comment. "It feels like we're being set up to take a huge fucking fall on this mission."

Jason sighed and nodded. "I'm not sure you're wrong, Joseph, but we've been tasked by POTUS."

"And since when do we care who appointed us to do the mission? Let's face it, if this were a private company, we'd tell them to pound sand." Joseph shook his head. "We have four Mercy

Teams, three of Jacob's teams, and four snipers going into a situation we have no solid intel about."

"That's not quite accurate." Jason reached for his tablet. "I received reports from Raven and Berserker this morning. They're on the ground."

"In France?" Jacob asked.

"No, in the war zone," Jason said. "Jinx and Rook are there, too, but I haven't heard anything from them as of this meeting."

"Who's in France?" Jacob asked.

"Viper, Phantom, Banshee, and Demon," Zane said from his seat beside Jewell.

"The entire class except Specter." Jacob leaned back.

"He's on a Mercy Team overwatch. The established Shadows are handling all missions until we have enough intel on this situation to handle it."

"What's the intel?" Joseph didn't care if the entire organization was deployed to the area. He wanted facts. Cold, hard facts they could use to make decisions.

"Check your inbox," Jason said, then waited for everyone to pull up the document.

"Our old friends." Joseph read the name of the radical dissidents he'd personally chased across Afghanistan and all points north, south, and east.

"Exactly. They want the war to continue. It brings attention to their political agenda and validates their existence in the eyes of their followers." Jacob nodded.

"Wait, this says they're actively recruiting martyrs?" Joseph snapped his eyes up to the screen. "Finally, an actionable item."

"What do you mean?" Jewell asked.

Joseph leaned forward to explain it to his sister. "These people will not drive through the gates of that venue with the dignitaries. If they're there to disrupt, blow up, kill, maim, or cause destruction, they'll get in other ways because security with the political representatives will be too tight."

"Such as housekeeping, deliveries, service personnel." Jacob was writing as he spoke.

"But won't they still have to get through security?" Jewell asked.

"They would, but this faction is known for making fake IDs. They've been able to get people inside areas you would think were airtight." Joseph had tracked a notorious member of the organization and finally found him dressed as a woman and working in a kitchen. The poison he dispersed at that wedding killed over thirty people. Joseph made sure he wouldn't kill another person.

Jason nodded. "So, we send this intel to the French government."

"And the Shadows on the ground in France," Joseph reminded him. "We can't divert all of our attention and resources to follow this information."

"True. It could be a misdirection," Jacob agreed.

"Or it could be a tangential attempt and not what we're looking for at all. Nothing indicates this faction had the resources to use, obtain, or purchase the threatened chemical or biological event that initiated this response," Jason said.

"What I don't understand is why isn't the French government telling us to shove off?" Joseph rubbed his forehead. "There's something we're missing."

"I believe you're correct," Jason said. "Jewell, I need you and Con to pass off the routine things to Ring and Brando. I want an in-depth review of every participant of this summit. I don't care how many rules you break to get me the information. I want to know what each person in each entourage eats for breakfast and when they shit every day."

Jewell made a sound of disgust. "Well, that's pretty detailed. It could take a hot minute."

"I don't care. If you need more help, we can

upgrade Honor for this mission. I know she's enjoying the work she's doing for Jared, but this is the priority, and she's met all our requirements and then some."

"I don't think that would be a bad thing. She has a team of four in New Orleans now, so she should be able to keep an eye on them and help us out, too. I'll call her after we get off here. I'll be happy to have her work with me, and if she can keep the clearance, then we could pull her in when things get tight."

"Done. Let her know." Jason looked up. "Is there anything else we need to discuss?"

Jacob nodded. "Yes. Scott Evers has worked his ass off up in South Dakota. The structures will be done in time for the familiarization training. According to Chief, the medical teams are working with Dr. Montrose, and we're at about fifty percent on acquiring the needed medical supplies. We'll need access to an airlift transport from South Dakota to France. It will be carrying all the equipment, medical supplies, and personnel."

Jason tapped something on his tablet and asked, "When will the teams arrive at the annex?"

"One month prior," Jacob replied. "I'll meet them there, and with Mike and Double D, we'll run them through the facility and make sure they have a damn good idea what they're up against."

"I'll be there, too," Joseph said. "This is a fucked-up mission. I don't like it. I don't want us involved in it. There's something here we're not seeing."

"Agreed. Thanatos will cover the Rose?" Jason took off his glasses and stared at the camera.

"Always." The assassin was his second in command and a damn good friend.

"All right. Jewell, start with the outliers, the contingents who are invited but not really participants." Jason shook his head. "I'm with Joseph on this. We aren't seeing the forest because of the tree in front of us. Give us an eagle's view. I've already initiated reinstatement of Honor's clearance."

"We'll do it," Jewell replied.

"Work the plan and dig deep. Archangel out."

Joseph cleared the video conference and stared at his dark computer screen. Two threats. One credible. That fucking faction would try something ... but damn it ... what were they missing? His gut told him something big, and his gut was never wrong.

CHAPTER 12

Lillian woke with a start. What in the world? The knocking on her apartment door sounded again. She stumbled out of bed and through the small front room. She pawed at the lock and opened the door. Billy smiled widely at her. No matter how sexy that smile was, it wasn't the time to flash it. "What do you want? It's the middle of the night."

"No, it isn't. It's five-thirty. I'll give you ten minutes to get ready for PT." He dropped down and planted a kiss on her forehead. "You're adorable in your jammies and all sleepy."

Lillian looked down and then back up at him. "That's because it's the middle of the night. We don't have to meet until seven."

"Ah, the teams don't. We're cadre. We work out before the teams." Billy put his hands on her shoulders and turned her around. "Running gear. Go." He gave her a gentle push. "Ten minutes."

Although she wasn't sure what she said, Lillian grumped something in reply and returned to her bedroom, where she shed her warm flannel pajamas. *So what if they had bunnies on them?* She put her hair up in a messy bun and shoved a couple of hairpins through it to make sure it stayed in place. Her running gear was already laid out. She yawned and headed into the bathroom to brush her teeth. The cold tile floor woke her up more than the knock on her door. She brushed her teeth, then headed back into the bedroom to put on her gear. She opened the door, and Billy was leaning against the wall, waiting for her.

She blinked at him. How had she not noticed how many muscles were on display? He wore running shorts and a t-shirt that was spray painted on. Damn. "I know I'm not quite awake yet, but aren't you dressed a bit too … little … to be running outside?" She waved at her joggers and lifted her insulated jacket.

"Well, if you want to run outside, we could, but

I'd rather hit the treadmill and then maybe lift some weights."

"There's an inside gym?" Lillian dropped her head back. "Why hasn't anyone told me that?"

Billy dropped his arm over her shoulders. "Did you ask?"

"Stop making sense. It's too early," she groaned as he moved her down the hallway. They walked into the common room and then entered a door she'd not opened. After about a two-minute walk, they entered a gymnasium. Ten treadmills, exercise bikes, weight machines of every kind, and a large selection of free weights. She recognized Adam, Mike, and the twins, who were doing pushups in the corner. Billy's friend Isaac was lifting weights in that area, and he nodded to them as they entered.

"I had no idea this was here."

She followed Billy to the treadmills. He got on one, and she shed her joggers, revealing her running shorts. "There is one above ground adjacent to the barracks."

"Why didn't I think to ask?" She looked at the panel on the treadmill and started the machine. She started off at a fast walk to warm up, and as soon as she felt good, she increased the speed to a steady jog. She loved to jog, but she was a fair-weather exerciser. If it were too cold, she found excuses to not put in the effort, which was why she gained five or ten pounds every winter and lost it as the weather warmed up.

Billy, on the other hand, ran. The pace he ran was ridiculously fast. She was the slowest turtle in the world compared to him. Isaac took the treadmill on the other side of Billy, and the belt on that machine turned just as fast. By the time she'd jogged two miles, all the men were on the treadmills, and they were all flat-out running.

"Yeah, I wish they were showing off, but they aren't."

Lillian grabbed the bars on the treadmill and hit the stop button. She glanced at the tiny woman next to her. "That's insane." Lillian pointed back at the men.

"Right?" The woman extended her hand. "I'm Joy. The twin closest to us is my husband."

She shook the woman's hand. "How can you tell them apart?" she joked.

"Believe me, there's a world of difference between the two." The woman nodded toward the weight machines. "Work out with me and leave these meatheads to do their macho thing."

"Thanks, don't mind if I do." Lillian picked up her joggers and insulated running jacket and followed Joy to machines she recognized.

"I'm going to be teaching your close-in-defense classes," Joy said as she racked an incredible amount of weight for her leg lifts.

"You are?" Lillian asked from the squat machine she was configuring so she wouldn't embarrass herself.

"Yep. Kind of my specialty," Joy said. "I learned early how to protect myself. Figure everyone needs to know, so when they ask me, I have no problem giving some insight into dirty fighting and how to take a bastard out."

Lillian stopped and stared at the woman. She wasn't just a wife who used the same gym as her husband. She stopped. Of course, she wasn't. She hadn't seen any spouses down there. There was the clearance issue. Everything dropped into place with that realization. "So, you work for Guardian, too?"

"I do, and no, I'm not at liberty to tell you in what capacity I work for them." The woman extended her legs, lifting the stack of weights.

"I'm learning to not ask." Lillian bent her legs and dropped down into a squat.

"Smart. Your specialty is bio protection, right?" Joy asked before she hefted the weights again.

"Sort of. I practiced as an infectious disease doctor, but with this mission, I'm learning to be a chem and bio protection specialist." She bent her knees again and slowly lowered into a squat position.

"Scary shit," Joy said as she lifted again.

"No kidding," Lillian agreed. They finished their reps, switched machines, adjusted the weights, and started another set. "They're still running." Lillian shook her head as she lifted a much smaller stack of weights than Joy did.

"They don't want to be the first to stop. It's a matter of pride. Stupid, competitive, man-pride." Joy bent down into a squat, then pressed up with perfect form.

"I'd rather be able to make it through the day without dying."

Joy grunted in what Lillian assumed was agreement. They worked out for half an hour, and although she didn't see which man stopped first, they were all off the treadmills when she and Joy were finished.

Billy walked over to her. "Are you ready?"

She looked at him suspiciously. "For what? I'm not doing the craziness you guys have been doing."

Billy laughed and shook his head. "No, to go back."

"Oh, then, yes, I am. Let me get my stuff." She walked back to where Joy and her husband were talking to gather her outside clothes. "Thanks for the workout."

"I'm here every morning," the woman said. "I'll see you."

"You will." Lillian smiled and caught up with Billy, who was making his way to the exit. "I like Joy. She's a straight shooter."

Billy chuckled. "You can say that again." He glanced at his watch. "How about I stop by in thirty minutes, and we'll go grab breakfast in the cafeteria topside. Then we'll hit the briefing Mike is doing."

"What's he briefing on?" She'd seen it on the schedule, but she had no idea if it were a welcome thing or what.

"Assigning overwatches to teams. Introducing them to each other and explaining in detail the familiarization classes they'll be required to take."

Lillian stopped. "Which team did you get?"

Billy couldn't hide a smile, and she grabbed him around the waist and hugged him. "I'm so glad."

He held her for a moment. "You didn't think I'd let someone else watch over you, did you?"

"I didn't know if we had a choice." She wiped off her cheek. "You are really sweaty."

"Happens when you exercise."

"Or when you have …" She paused, trying to recall what Joy called it. "… stupid, competitive, man-pride issues."

Billy threw back his head and laughed. "That's Joy talking."

"She's kind of right, though, isn't she?"

"I'll admit I *may* resemble that remark. The others, though, they *definitely* do." Billy took her hand, and they walked down the hall together.

He stopped in front of her door, turned to her, and dropped a kiss on her lips. "Thirty minutes?"

She nodded and watched him walk across the hall and enter his apartment. After opening her door, she shut it behind her and leaned against it with her eyes closed. The man's charisma enveloped her like a warm blanket. She was so comfortable with him. What was between them was easy and so good. Her eyes popped open. Maybe she could do casual. Maybe she could be happy with what she had right now instead of … She stood away from the door suddenly. "No, Dion, you *dick*, you are not welcome in my life anymore. I'm happy, and I will never let you hurt me again."

Lillian marched to the bathroom, stripping off her clothes as she went. "If I want to invite a man into my bed, I can. I can do it. *I* can be the woman *I* want to be." She turned on the shower and stepped under the water. And she could have the man she wanted, too. She smiled and closed her eyes. And boy, oh boy, she wanted Billy.

CHAPTER 13

Billy glanced at his watch again. According to her class schedule, they were supposed to be out by five. It was five-thirty now, and the chow hall only stayed open for another thirty minutes. He glanced at his watch again and then opened the door to the classroom. Lillian stopped talking and looked at him.

"Sorry, Doc, you need to let these people eat. Chow hall closes in thirty minutes."

Lillian's head whipped around as she glanced at the clock. "We'll pick this back up in the morning."

The medics picked up their papers and computers, and several muttered their appreciation to him as they left the classroom. When the classroom was empty, he walked in and let the door shut behind him. "Hope you're not mad."

She held up a finger as she was writing. When she finished, she turned a smile at him. "No, not at all. I need to set a timer or something."

"Good. Dinner time."

She glanced at the closed door. "Can we just pick up something downstairs?"

"I've got something better than that. This afternoon, I drove into Hollister and picked up two dinners to go. I have clam chowder in a sourdough bread bowl waiting for us in my apartment."

"Oh, tell me you have a Chardonnay, and I'll be forever grateful."

"No …" Billy sighed. "A Pinot Grigio." He'd asked three different women what type of wine to get and had received three different answers. So, he'd closed his eyes and grabbed a bottle.

"That is just as good," she said and grabbed her things.

"How did the first day go?"

"Well, we all have a medical background, but the doctors are getting up to speed a lot faster than the techs, so I have them working as a pair. We go over a topic at a more doctor-focused level, and in turn, the docs on the team explain it to the techs.

They know their partners better than anyone else, so this way, I don't talk down to anyone, and the techs don't feel slow for not getting higher-level information."

"What about Abe?" He wasn't comfortable her tech wasn't with her.

"He's well informed on everything we're going over. I've prepped the information he'll need to catch up. Some of the streamlined protocols and such, but even if he never received that information, I'd put him against anyone going through this course. He's that good."

Billy opened the door for her. Well, maybe he didn't want Abe there after all. That sounded a bit … "Do you love him?"

She jerked her head around. "Who?"

"Abe?"

"Well, yeah. Like a brother. Why?"

"Just now, it kind of sounded like you cared for him a bit more than a working relationship."

"Oh, I do. He's my brother from another mother. But there could never be anything sexual between us. That would be …" She shivered. "No, that's just … gross."

Feeling a bit more reassured, Billy laughed at her reaction. They walked outside and moved at a quick clip to the clinic. The weather had turned colder, and the wind was whipping at a sharp pace. Dixon told him that, according to Frank Marshall, it would probably be the last snowstorm of the season. Billy didn't doubt the old cowboy for a second.

When he reached her door, he took his opportunity to kiss her. He'd become addicted to the small tastes he'd been allowed to have of her. She was sweet yet held a spice that zinged all the way to his cock and pooled at the base of his spine. But he wouldn't rush the woman. He'd rather have blue balls and jack off in the shower than make her not trust him by moving too fast. When he lifted away, he sighed. "I'll open the wine and start warming up dinner. Come over when you're ready."

"I won't be long." She smiled at him and entered her apartment.

"Ah, so that's why you snagged her team's number," Specter said from just outside his doorway.

Billy looked at him and lifted an eyebrow. "And?"

Specter laughed and held up his hands. "No judgment, brother. Just putting all the dots in a row."

"Better get to dinner. Chow hall closes soon."

"I'm going to Asp's for dinner." Specter shut his door behind him.

"Watch out for the murder kitten," Billy said as he crossed the hallway.

Specter stopped and looked at him. "Say what now?"

"Ask Isaac. It's a hell of a story. I still have the scars." Billy laughed and shut his door behind him.

He opened the bottle of wine and put a second one in the fridge. The clam chowder he poured into a saucepan and warmed slowly on the stove. The bread was in the oven. He'd set the table before he went to her class. He glanced at the candle on the table. He'd picked it up at the small general store. He was pretty sure the store carried them for power outages and such, but ... He found a lighter and lit the squat white candle.

Cheesy? Maybe. She deserved so much better, but he had limited resources, and ... well, she knew how he rolled.

He walked to the door when he heard her soft knock. She'd changed into an off-the-shoulder sweater, black yoga pants, and a pair of fluffy slippers. "You look"—edible, delicious, sexy, enticing—"relaxed."

"I'm starting to decompress a bit. I normally take thirty minutes to myself and just let the day wash off. Oh, a glass of wine would help." She moved over to his couch, kicked off the slippers, and sat down, curling her feet under her. He poured her a glass before pouring a finger of bourbon for himself. He took them over to the couch and sat down beside her. She leaned into him and took a sip. "Oh, this is nice."

"I'm a lucky guesser, then. I had no idea what kind you'd like." He took a sip of his bourbon.

"What are you drinking?"

"Believe it or not, a Texas bourbon."

"Why wouldn't I believe it?"

"Well, some of us old fogies believe the best bourbon is made in Kentucky. But I tried this when I was in Texas recently, and it was damn good. So, I bought a bottle."

"You can tell the difference? Don't they all taste alike?"

He gave her an exaggerated frown., "Do all wines taste alike?"

She mimicked his expression. "Kind of. I'm not a big drinker. How old are you?"

Billy closed his eyes and dropped his head back

against the wall, making a decided *thunk* sound when it hit. "Prehistoric."

She laughed at him. "How old, exactly, are you? Are we talking Jurassic or Cretaceous period old?"

He opened his eyes and popped his head off the wall. "What's the oldest?"

She made a face, and her eyes batted back and forth for a few seconds before saying, "Ah, Cambrian?"

He frowned at her. "Is that a question or a statement?"

She laughed. "I wasn't aware there would be a test, so maybe a bit of both?"

"Well, I'm that old. How old are you?"

She gasped. "Don't you know it isn't polite to ask a lady her age?"

"I do, but I figured we were close enough friends I could ask." He took another sip of his drink.

"I'm thirty-eight. Now, barring any Mesozoic-era creatures popping out of the bedroom to attack us, how old are *you*?"

Billy mumbled his age under his breath.

"What?" She laughed. "You're going to have to be a bit clearer."

"Forty-five." He shot the remainder of his bourbon.

"Oh, damn. Sorry, I'm going to have to leave. That's too old for me." She put down her wine and moved to stand up. Billy grabbed her around the waist and pulled her back onto the couch. Her laughter, infectious and lighthearted, rang out through the room. She ended up in his lap and turned toward him. He held her close to him. "Make an exception, just for me."

"Will you make it worth my while?" She leaned forward and pressed her lips to his. *Well, hell, yes, he'd make it worth her while.* His hands slid up her back and held her against him. He took charge of the kiss. At the sweep of his tongue, she opened for him, and he may have groaned a bit. The feel of her on his lap, leaning into him and kissing him, was exquisite torture. He broke the kiss, but she followed his lips. *Message received, sweetheart.*

He let his hands find her sweater's bottom and travel under it. His eyes popped open when he didn't encounter a bra. She pulled away. "Why are you stopping?"

Billy cupped her cheek with a hand. "If you're sure, we could relocate and get comfortable."

She stood up and extended her hand. Well, damn,

the night was going way better than he'd thought it would. She led him to the bedroom. All the apartments were set up the same way, so she knew the way. She dropped his hand and walked to the bed. Turning around, she removed the sweater and slid out of her yoga pants. *Holy hell.* He swallowed hard and watched as she laid down on the bed.

"Are you going to join me or stand there all night?"

Her words jerked him out of the comatose state he'd fallen into. He whipped his shirt off over his head. Screw dealing with buttons. He toed off his boots as he unfastened his jeans. They both came off in mere seconds.

"Oh, you are magnificent," she purred as she crooked her finger at him. There was no way she needed to do that twice. He was on the mattress and crawling to her the next instant. He stopped at her knees and kissed one, then the other. She giggled and squirmed when his lips traveled north.

He lifted his eyes. "Sorry. I'm ticklish."

"Oh, not a problem." He dropped to her thigh again and growled as he sank. He blew a raspberry on her thigh, and she shrieked with laughter. "Brat! Stop that!" Her legs lifted under him, and she pushed him away. He caught her and pulled her with him, rolling her on top of him.

"Are you ticklish here?" He lifted his head and kissed her collarbone.

"No." She still had laughter in her voice as she answered.

"Here?" He lowered the kiss to her chest above her breast.

"No." Her breathless response came quietly.

He rolled her to their side and kissed his way to the top of her breast. His fingers found the nipple his lips weren't devouring. Lillian arched under him. Her hands found purchase in his hair, and she held him in place until he moved to the other breast.

Languidly, he continued, driving her insane before he moved back up to kiss her. Her arms entwined around his neck, holding him tight against her. Fuck, the sensation of her soft skin against his was intoxicating. She shifted, and her legs opened for him. He settled between them, not breaking their kiss.

She arched under him, urging him to enter her. He broke the kiss then. "I need a condom."

"No. I've got us covered." She grabbed his face

with both hands and brought him down for another kiss.

With that, he let his body take over. Fuck rational thought. He moved them, and while he kissed her, he entered her. The feeling of her hot, wet sex was unbelievably tight. He broke the kiss and groaned as he held still. If he moved, he'd lose it. God, she was incredible.

Her fingers traced his backbone, and when she reached his ass, she grabbed him and arched. He hilted and swore his eyes rolled so hard he could see his brain. "God. Woman, you're going to make me come."

"That's the idea."

He looked down at her. "Not until you do." He wanted to make her orgasm. He wanted to watch her disintegrate in front of him.

"You don't have to worry about me." She made a move to pull him down for a kiss.

He reared back. "The hell I don't." He dropped down on his elbows. "This is about both of us. It always will be." He kissed her and started to move. Some bastard had done that to her. He would show her how a real man made love to a woman.

He watched her and gauged her responses to how he touched her. Making her feel good had become his focus. She was his priority now. He sensed she liked it when he stroked a bit harder and faster. Adjusting her leg, he grabbed her behind the knee and pressed it toward her chest. She flushed and arched as her hands grabbed the sheets. He lifted the other leg and snapped his hips harder, feeling her trembling under him. Her head moved back and forth, and she grabbed his arms. He watched as the beautiful woman under him shattered. Her eyes popped open, and she gasped as she orgasmed. With that visual, he let himself go and came harder than he could ever remember. Dropping her legs, he fell to his elbows over the top of her, his forehead dropping to her chest.

Her hand found the back of his head. They stayed like that for a long minute, gathering air in their lungs. He finally lifted his head to look at her. She stared at him. He narrowed his eyes. "Why are you looking at me like I'm a bug under a microscope?"

She laughed. "I wasn't aware that was how I was looking at you."

"You were. Almost as if you were trying to figure out what kind of bug I was." He rolled to his side, propped his head up, and looked down at her. "I'm not a bug."

"No. You're not." She rolled onto her side and mimicked his position. "You're different, though."

Billy made a face and flopped back on his back. "That is not what a man wants to hear after sex."

She laughed and moved so she was lying on his chest, looking down at him. "I've never had a lover put me first."

He lifted his head. "You're joking."

She shrugged. "No."

"Then you've never been with a real man." He ran his fingers through her hair. "Sex should be fantastic for both people. Not just one."

She closed her eyes and sighed. "It was. Simply fantastic."

He sighed dramatically. "*That* is what a man wants to hear after sex."

She chuckled. "Did you enjoy yourself?"

He sat up, forcing her back. He caught her in his arms and held her. "There wasn't one second of time I didn't enjoy what we did. You are a beautiful, responsive, sexy woman. Never doubt I enjoy my time with you. I do. I swear it."

"I do." She stared up at him. "Do you smell that?"

"What?"

"Is something burning?"

He vaulted out of the bed and raced into the kitchen as she said the words. The bread. "Damn it."

He opened the oven and grabbed the pan. Mistake. "Ouch! Fuck!" The pan with the burning bread bowls hit the floor with a clatter. He hissed and shook his hand.

Lillian was beside him in an instant. "Let me see."

"It isn't bad." He glanced down at his fingers. They were red, but there were no blisters forming.

She moved him over toward the sink. "Hmmm … how about we let the doctor in the room determine—"

The shriek of the fire alarm sounded above them. Billy reached up and hit the reset button, but the damn thing kept blaring.

"Turn it off!" Lillian yelled as she covered her ears with her hands.

"I'm trying to!" Billy reached up and twisted the damn thing off its mount. It was connected by wiring. He yanked it, snapping the wire from the back of the alarm. The thing bleeped twice and then silenced.

Lillian looked around at the disaster in the kitchen and turned to him. She started to laugh.

Billy blinked at her, then realized how funny the situation was.

The annex's phone system rang, and he picked up the landline. "I burned dinner." He knew it would be someone checking on them. Lillian's laugh at his admission was impossible to miss.

"The alarm went offline," Ethan, the annex's computer specialist, said.

"Yeah, about that. Someone should probably come by tomorrow and wire it back into the ceiling."

Lillian laughed harder as she used a potholder to pick up the pan from the middle of the kitchen floor.

"I'll do that. Have a good night." Ethan chuckled, and the line went dead.

He hung up the phone. "Well, when I set out to make a night unforgettable, I go all in."

She walked to him and hugged him. "I can absolutely guarantee I'll never forget tonight."

He dropped for a kiss, and the fire alarm chirped. He rolled his eyes, and Lillian dissolved into giggles against him. He wrapped his arms around her and laughed. What else could he do?

CHAPTER 14

The shrill sound of an alarm woke her with a jolt. She launched into a sitting position and pushed her hair out of her face. "My watch alarm." Billy's gruff voice made her jerk in his direction and blink. *Oh*.

She dropped back, pulled the covers up to her neck, closed her eyes, and snuggled as close to him as humanly possible. "I don't want to work out."

He patted her shoulder. "Neither do I, but …"

"We worked out enough last night." They'd made love twice, and she was pleasantly achy and deliciously satisfied.

"And it was fabulous, but I don't think the muscles we used are the same ones we'll be training today." His voice rumbled under her ear.

She sighed. "I'm not convinced."

He laughed, and then the covers were gone. "Hey!" she squealed, grabbing at the blankets he'd flipped to the other side of the bed.

"Ten minutes, woman. I'll be back." He reached for the jeans he'd worn over to her apartment last night and put them on.

"I wonder if the alarm ever stopped beeping."

"Fucking fire alarm," Billy grumbled. Then he bent down and kissed her. "But I also love that thing. It got me into your bed all night long."

"You didn't need a fire alarm." She reminded him when he lifted from their kiss, and man, what a kiss it was. She sighed and flopped back down onto the pillow.

"Nine minutes. Inside workout, not outside," he said as he left the bedroom.

Lillian shifted through the dark as she got ready to work out. She'd had fun. Stopping for a moment, she cocked her head and thought about that. She'd had fun. She'd enjoyed Billy's company. His vow to take care of her while they were having sex had shocked her. That had never been her experience. If she managed to climax while her partner was getting off, it was good, but it had never been a priority for her partners. Billy was different. He was someone she could see herself being with in the long term. She blinked at the mirror looking at herself. "Don't get ahead of yourself. Take it one step at a time." One glorious, sexy, fun step at a time. She swallowed hard. No, she was running, and she prayed he'd catch her. She lowered her gaze. Somehow, she knew he would. There was something so special about him. Something so unique that she knew he'd be there for her every single time.

After cleaning up in the bathroom, she slipped into her running bra and sat on the edge of the bed to put on her running shoes. She'd slept like the dead next to him after they'd moved to her apartment. They endured the random bleeping of the fire alarm while they ate but decided enough was enough and walked across the hall to her place.

She slipped into her t-shirt and walked across the hall to knock on his door. "You're late," she said with her hand on her hip.

"I found out it had a battery. I may have thrown it into a wall to find that out, but no more beeps." He held up a nine-volt battery as evidence.

"Quite the handyman, aren't you?" She leaned on the doorjamb.

"I believe in caveman tactics if that's what

you're referring to." Billy adjusted his t-shirt as if it had a tie. "Shall we go?"

"Or we could stay here since the beeping is done." She really didn't want to work out. Other forms of cardio were much more interesting.

Billy closed his eyes, and she watched a full body shiver overtake him. He ran his hand through his hair, then shook his head, looking at her. "I can't believe I'm saying this, but … later. Tonight. Your place. Dinner and then …" He lifted his eyebrows a couple of times.

"Fire alarms?" she suggested.

"I'm never going to live that down, am I?" He motioned for them to leave.

"Never," she agreed. They visited and laughed all the way to the gym.

Mike met them at the door, where he plopped a red plastic fire hat on Billy's head. "The first person to set off the fire alarm in the annex, and that's a feat, my friend. We were under attack, and those suckers didn't go off."

A flash of light surprised her until she realized Dixon, or was it Drake, had taken a picture of Billy wearing the hat. Adam Cassidy laughed unabashedly.

"Har, har, assholes. I forgot about the bread in

the oven. Sue me." Billy took the hat off and looked at it. "Dude, this is awesome. I'm keeping it." He put it back on his head and grabbed her hand. "Cardio time."

She laughed as she followed him to the treadmills. Her cheeks hurt from smiling, and it wasn't even six in the morning.

LILLIAN STOPPED TALKING when her timer went off. It was a pink elephant timer Billy had bought for her online after he'd stopped her class from running over for the fifth or sixth time. She didn't carry her cell phone any longer and had lost track of time completely, So, she set the hilarious-looking timer at the beginning of every class, so he didn't need to interrupt and remind her to let the teams move on to the next class or eat. She glanced at the whiteboard. "We'll finish this up tomorrow."

One of the doctors raised his hand. "Lillian, I'm concerned. With this protocol, you're skipping several steps, and the damage that the gas can do won't be completely stopped."

She nodded and walked over to the whiteboard. "We are skipping them. On purpose."

Another doctor spoke up as she heard a knock on the door. "To expedite the removal from the contaminated area?"

She glanced at the door and waved Billy in as she answered the question. "Yes and no. With this protocol, we're minimizing the most damage for all situations under this umbrella with our available stock of products. I've worked with the leading experts in each of these fields and developed this scaled-down version to save as many lives as possible. We're in a difficult position. We can't know the extent of the exposure, so our mandate is to keep them alive and ship them to hospitals. The French government knows what we're preparing for and that they may need to handle an influx of any number of possibilities."

"So, wartime tagging?" one of the techs asked.

Lillian frowned. "Which means?"

Billy answered that. He sat on the edge of her desk, which was his usual perch. "When in a battlefield situation, the person is tagged with a code. Those who go first into surgery. Those who can wait, and those who the surgeons shouldn't waste their time on."

Lillian blinked at him. Damn, that was … cold. But she could see the need for it in a wartime scenario. That was basically what they were preparing for, wasn't it? "Right," the medic said. "Have we developed that type of system?"

"I haven't." Lillian looked at the tech. "Can you do it?"

The man blinked, then nodded. "Yeah, it wouldn't be difficult."

"How long would it take?" she asked.

"Give me a couple days. I need to make sure I account for all the scenarios we're going over."

"We have a few more to walk through, too." Lillian looked at the team. "I'll let Mike know we'll need tags, right?"

"I can let him know what type." Billy looked at the tech. "Color-coded, yellow, red, and black?"

The guy shook his head. "We'll need at least six, and with a few more protocols to cover, we'll have to use an Alphanumeric code."

"Just get it to Lillian when you have it constructed, and we'll get it ordered and produced." Billy looked back at her. "Sorry to interrupt."

"No problem. We're in uncharted waters, and any and all advice is welcome. And the elephant had just sounded, so we were wrapping up for the night," she said as the class started to break up.

"Good. Don't forget right after physical training tomorrow, we'll be doing our first familiarization class with your overwatches. The mock venue is close enough to finished that we can run scenarios before the teams arrive."

Lillian put her papers in order and picked them up, waiting for her contemporaries to leave. When the last was out of the door, she walked over to where Billy was sitting and kissed him. He pulled her into him and crushed her papers between them. She didn't care. When he released her, she looked down at the mess of yellow paper.

"You should probably go digital." He laughed as he helped her straighten the jumbled mess of notes.

"I've never been able to do that. My mind likes this, so I keep it."

"That makes sense." He stood and dropped his arm over her shoulders as they walked out of the classroom. "Dinner at my place tonight."

"Did you go into Hollister? How was your appointment with Dr. Wheeler?"

"I did go. It went well. He didn't schedule another and told me to call if I needed to talk. Oh, we're having paella."

"That sounds fantastic, both the talk with Dr. Wheeler and dinner. And did you get bread?"

He groaned. "Yes, but you're in charge of warming it up."

"I think the plaque the guys put up commemorating your fire alarm in the common room is very attractive."

"I didn't think they'd actually put one up, but yeah, I was rocking that hat." Billy laughed and opened the door for them. Spring had come to South Dakota. The snow had melted, and the days were warm. Shoots of green filled the pastures. The herds of cattle had calved, and little ones jumped and ran around mothers who seemed to tolerate the young ones' exuberance. "Did you have a good day?"

She nodded. "We have it pretty much down. A couple more protocols, but yeah, it was a good day. Soon, it will be just a repeat and reminder type of thing."

"Which is good. When the teams come in, the medics will need to be out there to watch how everyone works together. To know what to do and what not to do. Which reminds me, Abe needs to be recalled. Mike said he would do that tomorrow in case you wanted to call him first."

Lillian shook her head as they walked up the clinic's stairs. "No. His wife doesn't like me, so I think it would be better if it comes from Mike."

"Why doesn't she like you?" Billy held open the door for her; the concern on his face was genuine, and it made her feel warm and protected.

"Abe said she was jealous of me."

"Oh, okay. That makes sense," Billy said, following her into the clinic.

"What?"

"Who wouldn't be jealous of you? You're gorgeous."

She laughed. "That's what I said to Abe. But in reverse. If you ever saw Heather, you'd know she has nothing to be worried about as far as I'm concerned. She's gorgeous."

Billy shut the supply room door behind them and put a finger under her chin. "No one is more attractive than you. I'd fight anyone who says otherwise." He dipped down and brushed his lips against hers.

When he lifted away, she smiled at him. "You'd have to fight every man on this ranch. They all believe their wives are beautiful."

He winked at her. "Bring them on. I'll stand by my words."

They made their way down to the facility and walked toward the apartments. "What are we doing tomorrow?"

"We're going to show the teams the range, show them how we perform overwatch duties, and then go over some dos and don'ts." Billy escorted her to her door. He leaned down and kissed her. "Enjoy your decompression time. Come over when you're ready?"

"Be right there. I just want to grab a shower," she said before toeing up to kiss him. She shut the door behind her and leaned against it. Having Abe there would be good and bad. She loved the guy like a brother, but he was overprotective and could be an asshole sometimes. Either he and Billy would get along well, or they'd be like oil and water.

She put her notes down and stripped down to shower. She needed the time alone to process the day and adored the fact that Billy understood. As she stepped under the warm water, she closed her eyes. Time at the annex had been a whirlwind. She spent more time with Billy than she spent alone, and for once in her life, she was happy with that arrangement. She was very clear about her boundaries with him, and he'd never overstepped.

Leaning forward, she let the warm water pelt her shoulders, which were sore from the weights she'd lifted yesterday. She'd lost weight even though she was eating regularly. Thanks to her food monger. She smiled as the water streamed over her. She loved that guy.

Lillian blinked and lifted her head. As water streamed into her eyes, she stepped forward. Did she? She sat down on the tiled bench in the shower and stared at her feet. As she thought, the water swirled around them and made its way to the drain. She thought she'd fallen in love with Dion, but that was a toxic relationship. What she felt for him initially was an attraction and then desperation as he weaved his controlling and manipulative ways through her life.

But Billy … She smiled. He was everything Dion wasn't. He was caring and genuine. He was a protector, and he put her first. His sense of humor and hers meshed, and with him, being happy was easy. And she *was* happy. The joy that filled her was real. She loved Billy but was stuck between a rock and a hard place. She was the one who had stipulated they stay casual. Did he even want something more? When had she walked over that ledge? When had she fallen for the cute guy with the quick wit and ready smile? And then there was a matter of location. He lived there. Her life was in the Pacific Northwest.

"Stop. Slow down. You don't need to make any decisions today." *Or tomorrow,* she added silently. With their relationship, she would be methodical, and even though she'd made herself vulnerable again, she could take the time to be comfortable with what was happening. Nothing needed to be decided immediately.

She finished her shower and combed her hair before slipping into a pair of yoga pants and a too-big t-shirt. "Just relax. You don't even know how he feels." She slid into her slippers. "And if he feels the same way, then you can go slowly." She nodded to herself. *But how would she know?* "Stop. Just stop. Go have dinner and be with the man you love, whether or not he loves you." She glanced at her reflection in the mirror, made a face, then headed across the hall. The door was unlocked, and she walked in. "That smells heavenly."

"Ciera, Scott's wife, makes it. I swore I was in Spain the first time I had it." He nodded to the bread on the sheet pan. "The oven is on. Your wine is on the counter."

She laughed and put the bread into the oven. "Chicken."

"Nope. If we get distracted, and the bread burns, you can wear the fire hat and have a plaque dedicated to you." He leaned over and kissed her. "Just sharing the wealth."

"And I'm so grateful for the privilege," she said as she took his glass of wine from him instead of retrieving her own. "How was your day?"

"It was good. I worked with Specter and was able to teach him a trick he hadn't seen before. We sent lead downrange and have been practicing at the mock venue. We've decided overwatch positions based on dividing the area into four sectors. I'm assuming four teams, four sectors of responsibilities, right?" He looked over at her as he turned off the burner under the rice dish.

"That would be the commonsense way to deploy, yes."

"That's what we figured, too. We'll show the groups where they'll be assigned tomorrow. Of course, that could be changed when Alpha arrives and starts work with the teams."

Lillian put the silverware on the table, then headed back to the cupboard for dishes. "Why would it be changed?"

"He's in charge of the teams and their positioning. There are only three of those teams, so someone will do extra duty, or, they may assign three sectors and have one medical team float. That overwatch would need to be in the center of the venue, and there's a place where we can see almost all the grounds. It would be a hell of a shot if we needed to fire, but we're good enough."

"Who's the best?" she asked when she set the bowls beside him.

"Coin toss between Alex, Asp, and me. Specter is damn good, but he's young and needs more lead through the barrel before he's as good as us. He'll be closer to his team. He's accepted that restriction. But I wouldn't want him hunting me. He works at his skill every day. His accuracy is crazy good, and his accuracy at extreme distances is getting better as he practices."

She blinked. *Wait, what?* "Hunting you? Why would Specter hunt you?"

Billy looked over at her and gave her that half grin. "That's just a saying."

"Oh." She laughed. "Thank goodness. Anyway, when will the teams be here?"

"Two days. Why?" He handed her an oven mitt and carried the paella to the table.

She retrieved the bread and put it on a cutting board. "Cash will be here. Have you met him? He's Foxtrot Team leader. He's Abe's brother."

"Cash? You mean Costello?" Billy threw back his head and laughed. "Yeah, I know him. The man is insane."

Lillian smiled as he pulled out her chair for her to sit down. "He's that for sure. He kind of reminds me of you."

"What? No way. I'm a smartass. He's an insane ass." Billy sat down. "There's a difference."

Lillian cut the bread as he dished out the rice. "Too much," she said as he put another spoonful on her plate.

"But you needed some shrimp. Protein." He pointed to the one shrimp he'd put on her plate with the heaping scoop of rice.

"Ah, what about all of these?" she asked, pointing to the abundance of shrimp already on her plate.

"You should eat those, too." He smiled and leaned over for a kiss.

"You'll make me fat," she said as he lifted away.

"Not possible, and I wouldn't care. I love all of you, no matter the size." He shoved a forkful of rice into his mouth and froze. His eyes slid in her direction.

She felt a lightning bolt of emotion sizzle through her at his words. He loved all of her. Her eyes widened, and she looked at him. Yeah, he had that *Oh, shit* look on his face. She reached for her wine glass and lowered her gaze. "Bet you wish you could take that back, don't you?"

He put his fork down and turned his chair toward her. Leaning forward, he placed his elbows on his knees. "Lillian, look at me, please."

She glanced at him. "It's okay. You can take it back. I understand. After all, I was the one who said we needed to keep it casual, you know." She lifted the wine glass to her lips. Her hand shook so badly the wine sloshed in the bowl of her glass.

He carefully took the glass from her trembling hands and put it on the table with a delicate clink before dropping to his knees beside her. His eyes showed a storm of emotions. "I meant what I said just now, and yeah, I know it's way too early to be saying the words. I know what healthy relationships *aren't*. I know you do, too. This, what's between us, isn't that. This is good, and it's right. I'm at peace with how I feel about you and me together. It feels so damn good." When she started to speak, he held up a hand, stilling her. "You don't have to feel the same way right now or, for that matter, ever. I learned I'm not responsible for how you feel, only for how I do. It was a hard lesson that took far too many years to learn." With a slow, reverent motion, he lifted her hand, placing it over his heart. She could feel the way it pounded against his chest. "I want only the best for you. Maybe I'm not that. You get to decide how you feel about me. My heart, my life, is yours if you want it."

Lillian swallowed hard. "I know this is good. I know it's right. But so many things …" She closed her eyes and shook her head slightly to dispel the whirlwind of thoughts. "No." She opened her eyes and watched as he seemed to diminish in front of her. She grabbed his face with both hands. "I love you. I need you to know that. I do. This is just so fast."

A hopeful smile broke through that apprehensive gaze. He leaned closer, closing the gap between them. "Fast isn't always bad."

"But it is scary. To me, *this* fast is almost terrifying." She shook her head. "We need to slow down."

"I can do that. But I'll still show you how right this is." He kissed her gently.

"You already have," she whispered when he pulled away. "Just give me time to get it all straight"— she tapped her temple—"up here."

"I'll give you until the last star falls from the heavens. Oh, man … I rolled my eyes so hard just now at that corny line I saw my brain." He gently placed his forehead against hers, and their combined laughter mingled in a dance of relief.

Lillian spoke when the laughter started to fade. "I don't think seeing your brain is possible."

He pulled away and gave her an odd look. "Are you sure? I do it routinely."

She wrapped her arms around his neck and hugged him. "I'm pretty sure. I love you."

He stood up and held his hand out to her. "I understand this can be rewarmed."

She lifted out of her chair. "Is that so? Seafood?"

He looked at the table and tugged her in the direction of the bedroom. "I have microwave popcorn."

She chuckled. "Gourmet fare."

"Nope, but I'll melt extra butter and add some parmesan cheese, then it'll be gourmet." He kissed her, and they started to move. The soft click of the bedroom door as he backed her through it told her where they were. Their hushed, slow, footsteps on the carpet intensified her anticipation. He shut the door to the bedroom and backed her toward the bed as he lowered for a kiss, and she wrapped her arms around his neck.

Her back pressed into the soft bedding, and she relaxed under his weight. The intimacy between them had never been awkward. She ran her hands over his shoulders and plucked at the material as he kissed her. Breaking the contact, he lifted up and whipped off the offending material, tossing it somewhere beyond the bed. She reached for his belt and unfastened it. "This, too."

"Nope." Billy smiled at her. "Your turn." She held his gaze as she crossed her arms, found the hem of her shirt, and pulled it off. Her hair scattered in a thousand directions over the pillow.

Billy reached down and touched a lock. "A halo," he whispered. She reached for his hand. "I'm not an angel."

He blinked and cocked his head. "You don't understand, do you? To me, you are an angel. You shined a light on the darkest places in my soul and forced all the old demons out."

"How did I do that?" She barely breathed the question.

"By existing." He lowered and swept her lips with his. "Simply by existing."

Her breath caught at the depth of emotion flooding over her. She arched under his touch and let her hands travel over his body, boldly claiming what she knew was hers.

Clothes became a hindrance, and skin found skin. She lifted her leg, and he delved lower. His kisses and small nips made her skin dance under his onslaught. Feeling became the only need. She felt his tongue and fingers as they teased her core. The sensations pulsed with his movements. She rocked her hips until he draped an arm over them, steadying her. Her body ached and trembled. Finding his hair with her fingers, she twisted it in her grip. Billy's touch pulled her tighter and tighter until she snapped, and the most wonderful repeating percussion of sensation radiated from her core. Her orgasm rippled and waned. She opened her eyes and found him looking down at her. "You are an angel, my angel."

She lifted a hand to his cheek and pulled him down to her. "I love you." She lifted her knees, and he settled between her legs. When they kissed, he entered her, and she moaned at the feeling of him filling her so completely.

As he lifted to his elbows, she stared at the man above her. Magnificent. His defined muscles moved under his skin. He slowed and dropped for another kiss, his hips moving as their tongues danced. Her fingers traced his back, trailing along his spine, and she gasped a bit when he shifted his weight. His eyes opened, and a wicked smile appeared. "You like that?"

"Yeah," she puffed.

"Yeah?" He did it again, and she arched under him. She gripped his shoulders as he moved and that amazing sensation built again. Her body tightened until she shattered. Above her, Billy finished, his long groan as he climaxed as raw and basic as her response. He settled on top of her, holding most of his weight on his elbows.

She ran her fingers through his sweat-dampened hair. After they caught their breath, he rolled to the side, and she turned to him. "How did we get so lucky? Finding each other out here in the middle of nowhere?"

He stared at her for a moment. "I don't know, and I don't care. Whatever forces brought us together … it doesn't matter. What matters is we never let these feelings go."

"I'll hold on as tight as humanly possible." She pushed his damp bangs away from his eyes.

"And I'll never let go. I love you, Lillian, and that love is forever."

He moved to kiss her, but her stomach rumbled. Billy looked down at her abdomen and then up at her. "Gourmet popcorn time?"

"Sounds fabulous." She laughed when he bounced out of the bed and headed to the kitchen naked. "Just don't burn it!"

"Har, har, har, woman!" he called back. "Come out here, and I'll slather butter all over you."

Lillian's eyes popped open, and she laughed and scrambled out of bed. "Don't tempt me with a good time!"

CHAPTER 15

"Welcome to our home away from home," Billy said as the medics finished the long walk to the firing range. "Each of you will need a pair of ear protectors and safety glasses."

He waited for each to don their safety gear. "Along here, you'll see four observation posts. Each team will share one. We'll show you what we are capable of doing as your overwatches, and then we'll go into what you should or shouldn't do to help us do our job." He paused, then continued, "I need each person to look through the scope and identify the orange target. Does everyone have it?" He waited until all the teams located the orange target.

"How far away is it?" one of the medical technicians asked.

"Eight hundred meters or over eight football fields away," Asp supplied.

One of the docs lifted onto his toes and shielded his eyes. "I can't even see it without the scope."

"We'll do this four times. I have the north, which is the head." Billy moved to his weapon and laid down. He lowered, tucked the weapon, and drew a deep breath. He released it, drew another breath, released half, and then slowly squeezed the trigger. He ejected the round, grounded his weapon, pocketed the brass, and stood up.

He heard the mumbled comments but moved over to stand with Lillian, who had her own scope. "That was good." She smiled up at him.

"The distance isn't that far. We're proficient up to eighteen hundred meters, although the weapon's makers only guarantee thirteen hundred meters."

"Proficient?" She laughed at him.

"Okay, so I'm humble. How about we won't miss?"

Asp was down next. "I have south. Guess where my shot's going."

The man fired, and Billy heard several of the men watching groan. Lillian frowned and looked through the scope. "Oh, that would hurt."

"Groin shot," another doctor said. "Brutal."

"I have east," Alex said and slowly got into position. He turned his head to the medics behind him when he was down. "On the day of our mission, I'll be in position. There will be no delay. My leg does not affect my shooting ability." He moved into position and stated, "On the right line." His shot rang out, and everyone ducked to the scopes.

"Damn. Right in the middle of the line."

Specter lowered to where his weapon waited. "I'm west. On the line as well." He tucked his weapon and fired.

"Damn. How many bullets do you guys shoot to get this good?" Billy recognized the med tech who was doing the tags for Lillian.

"Thousands," Asp said. "Now that you know we can shoot and we can choose where we land a bullet, there are a few things you can do that will make our jobs easier. The first would be if you hear the sound of gunfire or if something blows up, drop to the ground. Literally, drop like a rag doll and stay the hell down. If someone is shooting at you, it makes you less of a target. It also allows us to know you're out of our line of sight and out of the danger of our bullets."

"Got it. Stop, drop, and don't roll," one of the doctors said.

"Exactly." Alex nodded.

"But," Billy said as he stepped away from where Lillian stood, "if, for some reason, you're being held by a bad guy." He grabbed Asp from behind and held him so only his head was showing beside Asp's, using the guy as a human shield. "Don't move. Don't try to fight, don't try to drop, just stand still."

A red light appeared on his forehead. Everyone turned around and saw Specter at the top of the berm with his weapon trained on Billy. Billy spoke again, "If you move and he takes the shot, you could be killed." Asp moved, and they shifted, showing the red light now on his head. "If you drop and the bad guy lowers, the bullet will go over him and into whoever is behind him." Asp dropped down, pulling Billy with him. They resumed their position. "But if you hold still, freeze, and don't move a muscle, the bad guy will disappear."

"Bang," Specter said, and Billy dropped, freeing Asp.

"Jesus. That's just a few inches," one of the docs said.

"We live in a world of a fraction of inches, minute calibrations for wind speed and direction, adjustments for humidity, and the drop of the bullet. We know what our ammo will and won't do. What we don't know is what *you'll* do. So, that's the purpose of this class," Billy concluded.

"Our job is to protect you. Your job is to help us," Alex said. "Can anyone locate the red target?"

It took a moment, and Asp and Billy helped those who couldn't find it. "That's thirteen hundred meters." They did another round of shots, with each of them taking a different location. That time, he and Asp landed the east and west shots, and Alex and Specter took the north and south. There wasn't even a fraction of an inch difference between the eight-hundred-meter and thirteen-hundred-meter targets.

"Now, we'll load up into the van and make our way out to the mock venue. We'll show you where we'll likely be while we're working to protect you," Asp said. "Remember, these locations are subject to change depending on the setup of the teams that will be on the outside cordon and in the primary building with the participants, hopefully keeping the bad guys away from us."

They all piled into the fifteen-passenger van. "So, the rationale for this demonstration is informational?" one of the doctors asked.

Billy nodded as he started the van. "That's what we're hoping. But we prepare for the worst and ..."

"Hope for the best," several of the medical personnel said together.

"Whatever it takes, man," Asp said.

"As long as it takes," the entire van answered.

The trip took about twenty minutes, and the road was bumpy as hell, but when they got to the remote location on the ranch, Billy was impressed. The structures were bare bones, but they were exactly what they needed.

"Welcome to Paris," he said as everyone piled out of the van. "This is an exact duplicate of the venue where this historic peace accord will be signed. As you can see here," he pointed to a fence constructed of metal poles and crime scene tape, "a fence surrounds the buildings. In Paris, this fence is constructed of stone and is over six feet tall. We'll show you pictures when we get back to the classroom."

"Let's walk the property," Asp said, taking over

the class. Billy dropped to the back of the crowd with Lillian. She leaned into him when he put his arm over her shoulders. “Where will you be?”

“If we go with four sectors, I’ll be on the top of that building.” He pointed to the right of the gate where the vehicles would be entering. “That’s the hot spot. That’s where the dignitaries will enter the building and leave. The other areas are tucked behind this building.”

Lillian stopped and looked. “And if there are only three sectors?”

“Then under the dome on this building. I’ll have almost three-hundred-sixty-degree access. You’ll be the team that will respond if someone needs you. Site supervisor.”

She nodded, and they started walking to catch up with the rest of the medics. “That’s what Mike and I discussed, yes. Which way do you think Alpha will set it up?”

“I’m sure he’ll get the team's inputs, but from my simplistic way of thinking, three sectors. A roaming supervisor and a second overwatch moving to the affected area with the supervisor makes sense.”

She was quiet for a moment. “I hope this is all for naught.”

"We'll get the latest information when Alpha arrives." He hoped so, too.

She chuckled quietly. "That sounds like you don't think this will be for nothing."

"If there weren't a threat, Guardian would have figured it out by now." What he wanted to know was what exactly the threat entailed because the wide range of possibilities sucked. "I'm going into this knowing I may have to do my job, and so should you."

"I know." She stopped and waited until the crowd had gone ahead a bit. "I'm sure Abe will be here soon. You'll tell him what you told the others today?"

Billy frowned. "Of course, why?"

She shook her head. "That's the past raising its head again. Dion hated Abe."

"You like him. He has to be a good guy. Besides, I know his brother. They can't be that different."

Lillian laughed. "Boy, howdy, are you going to be surprised."

"I very well could be, but you know what, both Abe and I want you to be happy, so we'll figure it out if there are any tensions." He nodded to the group ahead of them. "We should catch up."

He clasped her hand, and they walked on to

catch up with the group. Billy examined every inch of the compound. It was smaller than he thought when he was reviewing the photos, but that always seemed to be the case. Scott Evers said the measurements were precise to the ones he was given. He turned and assessed each of the sniper's strongholds, recalling the protection of each from the photos they'd received from advance people on the ground. Some were hazy and taken from a distance, but the locations they'd selected were the best for their safety and the medical crew's overwatch.

The tour lasted another two hours, with the medics talking about three sectors versus four. Specter went back to the classroom for the photos, and the medics talked about logistics and care of patients for entrance and exit from the compound.

"We could bottleneck at the front," one of the doctors said. "What's the likelihood of a secondary entrance being opened?" He pointed to the back fence line. "That looks like a gate, doesn't it? We could bring ambulances in through this gate and out through that one."

Asp considered the pictures and looked at the mock-ups of the buildings. "That won't work. See here in the photos? Raised stone beds."

Everyone examined the photos that were now on the hood of the van. "What about taking them around the front building to the right and back?" Lillian drew the route with her finger.

Everyone leaned in to get a look at what she was talking about. "That could work. We'll need measurements," Alex said and glanced at Asp. "We could do a one in and one out at the front gate if we can't get the back gate opened."

"Traffic in and out would be the French police's responsibility. I can't imagine what a snarl it'll be if something goes down."

"We'll bring those suggestions up to Alpha. But now, it's time to wrap it up." Billy glanced at his watch. "Unless you want to miss dinner."

The class didn't move quickly. Several still looked at the photos as they drove back. The mood wasn't jovial as the realization of the mission grew heavier. Billy knew that feeling. He would be watching over the woman he loved. He'd never been more serious about learning every iota of information he could gather.

CHAPTER 16

Billy sat down at the conference table in the communication room. The room was secure but aboveground, so the team leaders could be included. They had the clearance to be underground but not the need to know, so they were being housed topside with the medics. It would be standing room only soon. He stood up and got Lillian's attention when he saw her at the door. The men parted to allow her in.

"Lillian!" Cash Costello shouted. He shoved through the crowd and picked her up, hugging her tight.

"Put me down, you oaf." She laughed as he spun her, almost taking out two of his team in the process.

As he put her down, he asked, "Where's Abe?"

"He'll be here tomorrow," she said. "We gave him as much time with Heather as possible."

"Man, that boy always finds the easy way out." Cash dropped an arm over her shoulders. "Come stand back here with the guys and me."

"Actually …" Lillian pointed over to him, and Billy winked at her, making her blush and smile back.

"Oh," Cash said, then removed his arm from her shoulders. He made a face and looked at Billy, too. "Oh, damn. Sorry about that, Pearson."

"No worries, Costello," Billy said, pulling Lillian's chair out. She made her way to her seat, and he slid it forward before he sat down.

Asp leaned over and said to Lillian, "You'll still be able to make the party, right?"

Lillian nodded. "Abe is coming in sometime in the morning. I'll get him up to speed. We'll be there." She smiled wide. "I'm looking forward to it."

"Lady and gentlemen," Mike White Cloud greeted as he entered the front of the room. The room went silent. "Alpha and Fury are here with the latest intel update."

Jacob King walked into the room. Billy had

never seen him in person, and the guy was a physical clone of his older brother, who stood beside him. "All right. We've had people on the ground in the Middle East and France. There has been a lot of misinformation and dead ends, but we finally have some actionable information."

"Like, why we're doing the job the French should be doing?" Cash said from the back of the room.

"Costello?" Jacob King looked up from the tablet he was holding.

"Yes, sir."

"Yeah, we have that information, too. Just put your motor in neutral for a minute, Mario, and let me do this briefing." He looked to Cash's right to his team. "If he opens his mouth before I'm done, someone slap a gag on him?"

There was laughter from that corner of the room, and Billy liked the good-natured comradery between Alpha and his teams. "We'll start with the intel from the Middle East."

Fury walked back to the screen that now had a map of the current conflict. "We now believe we have a two-pronged threat. The first one we'll talk about is the extremist group the An-Nour Al-Muqawama, or the Light of Resistance. They've been heavily recruiting personnel and filtering them to France. We believe the intent is to have them infiltrate the events leading up to the signing of the peace treaty or the event itself. Low-level workers, cooks, delivery personnel, cleaners, any way they can get close to the key political participants. This faction has had success with copying documentation, making it appear authentic but switching out the actual person with their operative. They have an economic and political stake in making sure this treaty does not get signed.

"The General Directorate for Internal Security has been apprised and is getting real-time updates from us. Some of our sources are working with both the Internal and External Security Directorates, so all bases are covered. We've made some advancements in gaining intelligence. We anticipate this operation will be impacted to some degree by whatever plans the Light of Resistance is planning."

"What's their general MO?" Dutch Kaiser, Echo Team leader, asked.

"Blow shit up and cause general terror." Fury shrugged. "Disrupting the event is the general consensus. So, you'll need to be on the lookout for anything suspicious inside the venue.

Anything out of place. A cook near a car. A delivery person unescorted. A truck parked without a driver or attendant. You know the drill."

Billy nodded. Terrorism 101.

"The second threat is less concrete." Alpha took over. "We've been receiving intelligence, not from the Middle East, but from our sources in Europe. We believe we have the target identified but need verification. We're working on that."

"Targeted how?" Billy asked.

Alpha put his hands on his hips and sighed. "That's the thing. What we have doesn't make sense. We've run it through our computers, and there's nothing we can find on the substance our source believes will be used."

"What's the substance, sir?" Lillian asked from beside him.

"Our informant called it Tarmilse Variant Bravo."

Billy watched as Lillian swayed, and her hands hit the table. "What did you call it? Repeat that, please."

Alpha frowned, picked up his tablet, and read the words. "Tarmilse Variant Two."

"No. God, no." Lillian stood up.

"Do you know what this is? There isn't any information on it anywhere." Fury leaned forward.

Lillian nodded. Her hand went over her mouth. "I can't believe it. It can't be."

"Dr. Montrose, do you know what this substance is?"

Lillian drew a shaky breath. "I believe I do, sir, but I signed some documentation that prohibits me from talking about it."

Fury leaned forward and growled, "Fuck the documents. We have a real-world threat. Spill the beans, Doc."

Billy stood up and moved in front of Lillian. "Perhaps you could clear the room, sir. Then maybe we could get some answers."

Fury looked at the rest of the people in the room. "Get out. Now."

Fury looked at Billy. "That goes for you, too."

"No, sir." Billy stood his ground. "I go where she does."

"We'll be waiting in the barracks area." Mike shut the door after the last person walked out of the conference room.

"Sir, I signed a non-disclosure statement with Plume. If I talk about this, they could sue me."

"Guardian will handle all of that," Alpha said as

he sat down. “If they come after you, they’ll have to go through us, and I can guarantee you that won’t happen.”

She looked at Billy, and he put his hand over hers. “They’ve never lied to me. You’ll be protected.” If not by Guardian, by him. They could disappear. He sure as hell knew how to do that, thanks to the fucking CIA.

She nodded. “This goes back five years. I worked at Plume Research Laboratories at the time. Dion Francis, the doctor I worked with there—”

“Dion the Dick?” Billy interrupted her. She’d told him about the bastard. Bits and pieces, but Abe’s moniker for the fucker stuck in his head.

She looked over at him and gave a half smile. “Yes.” She turned back to Alpha and Fury. “In full disclosure, at the time he was there, I was in an … intimate relationship with him.”

Alpha nodded. “Go on.”

“Dion was working on Tarmilse. It was a substance he was developing that was thought to have a therapeutic application. Only it wasn’t what it was supposed to be. That’s what got him fired.”

“So, this is a drug?” Fury asked.

“In essence, no. The mutation he was working

on was supposed to be used as a vector to deliver functional genes. Functional genes, or gene inactivation, can kill cancer and stop tumors from growing or metastasizing."

"So, it's a virus?"

She made a wavering motion with her hand. "Not a live virus, or it wasn't supposed to be. Dion's work turned out to be a live virus, though. According to the information I was able to access, the virus destroyed healthy cells of the respiratory tract in a rapid and mutated way."

"Why was he fired?" Alpha asked.

Lillian sat down and pulled her hands through her hair. "Dear God, will this man ever be out of my life?"

Billy rubbed his hand softly on her back, encouraging her to continue. She seemed to relax under his touch.

"I read some of his test results. The relationship we had was toxic, and he ... well, it was bad. I knew I had to tell someone when I saw what he was doing. I took pictures of the report with my phone and took it to our supervisor, who sent it to the board of directors. To make a long and horrid story short, he was told to stand down and assume another avenue of research. Not that nice. It came with a reprimand and a fine. A sizeable one. Six months later, he presented others' research to the board to show he'd done as they'd asked, but he'd continued to work on Tarmilse, making it more effective in the destruction of healthy cells. He was caught again."

Fury made a growling noise. "The fucker should have been fired the first time."

Lillian huffed a small laugh. "That time, he couldn't talk his way out of it. The Board did a surprise inspection of the facility. He couldn't hide what he was working on. His license was stripped from him, and he was excommunicated from the medical world. It was a huge mess."

"Is there a cure for what he's done?"

"Sir, I don't know if *he* is actually the one working on what you called a Bravo version. I can't tell you what this strain of virus will do or what it won't do. I didn't know that much then, and I know even less now."

Alpha leaned forward. "How would you suggest we proceed?"

"You'd need to contact Plume. We were told all his work was vaulted."

"What does that mean?" Fury asked.

"Locked up, sir. It's where research that could

harm people ends up. Out of reach and never to be seen again."

"Obviously this …"

"Dion Francis, sir," Lillian supplied the doctor's name again.

"*Asshat* didn't give all his notes to Plume." Fury's lip curved up in a snarl.

"Or perhaps Plume's vault isn't as strong as it should be," Billy suggested.

"True." Alpha drummed his fingers against the table. "Dr. Montrose, how long would it take to make an antidote or vaccine for this virus if there isn't already one?"

Lillian sighed and shook her head. "I'm not that type of doctor. I don't know. My research wasn't in the same area or as advanced as his. The little I remember of what I saw, it was a cross strain of some type. But I couldn't tell you what strains or how he mutated them. Plume would be where you need to go for the answers, sir."

"Given what information you do remember, would any of the remedies you've prepared for this mission work in combating the progress of this virus?"

Lillian stared at the table as she thought. Billy kept his hand on her back, wishing he could help but hoping being there was enough. Finally, she shook her head. "I'm not sure, sir. We have remedies for chemical and biological events. I'd have to know what the virus was at the end of his tenure, and then it would be a wild guess as to where it is now. Some of the underlying markers of the virus could be the same." She shook her head. "There are so many better qualified to answer those questions, sir. I'm not the person you need to ask, but I can recommend some of the most brilliant minds in the field."

Alpha stood up. "Do that. We'll get to work. And whether or not you believe it, Dr. Montrose, you've forwarded our intelligence gathering tenfold today. Plume will not come after you. Not after we're done with them."

Lillian nodded as the brothers walked out. When the door closed, she dropped her head to the table. "How can he be still screwing with my life?"

"Don't let him," Billy said from beside her.

Her head popped off the table, and she turned to look at him. "Babe, real enemies I can defeat. How can I fight a ghost from the past? How can I defend my Guardians from him?"

Billy smiled. "Your Guardians?"

She frowned. "Yes, every Guardian entrusted

into our care belongs to us. We are responsible for them, their health, and, ultimately, their lives."

Billy smiled at her. "That's exactly what I say to myself on every overwatch mission."

She leaned into him, whispering, "Will our ghosts ever disappear?"

"Mine has. Yours will. What's happening now will ensure he won't bother you or anyone else again." Guardian would make sure he was incarcerated or stopped if he were, in fact, the one working on the virus.

JACOB AND JOSEPH KING walked into CCS. The growl of a large dog stopped them in their tracks.

Jacob's eyes flicked to the right. There in the corner was a dark gray wolf with blue eyes. "Ethan?"

Ethan came out of the small kitchen area. "Oh, hey. Come on in."

"Not until you call off the hellhound." Joseph didn't so much as move a muscle.

"Thor, it's okay, bud," Ethan said to the dog, tossing him a piece of popcorn. The dog effortlessly caught the kernel and laid back down. "He's good." Ethan plopped down into a huge computer chair. "What's up?"

"Need a secure conference with Jewell and Archangel," Joseph said. "Shouldn't he be outside?" He pointed at the wolf, who bared his teeth at Joseph.

"No, he's fine. I run with him in the morning, Grandpa Frank takes him out with him on a ride at lunch, and either Lizzy or Kadey, sometimes both, call me, and I send him up so they can play with him after school. When I'm done for the day, we find something to do. Fetch or chasing rabbits."

"Wait, you let those girls play with that dog?" Joseph arched an eyebrow.

"Sure, he's a good boy." As Ethan spoke, the dog's tail thumped the ground, and he rolled onto his side. He let out a big sigh and closed his eyes.

"Jewell, need to conference in you and Archangel," Ethan said as his fingers typed. "Nope. Alpha and Fury." Ethan laughed. "Yeah, he did. Does Dude?" Ethan glanced at Joseph. "I'm putting you on video and speaker."

Jewell looked up at the camera and waved. "Hiya! Jason is just finishing up a meeting. Anything I can do before he gets here?"

"Can you find any information on Dion Francis? He's a doctor who used to work for Plume Laboratories." Jacob sat down in one of the chairs at the table in front of the video screen where Jewell was shown.

"Ethan, pan for the usual. I'll go to the dark web."

"Dark web, why?" Joseph asked as he sat down.

"Well, for starters, I'll find his social faster than trying to get into the government agencies to do it," Jewell said as her fingers flew across the keyboard. "Second, any address he had or currently has will be listed along with any credit card information that may have been shifted from reputable sources with shit firewalls."

"There are fifty-seven Dion Francis listings in NCIC," Ethan said as he worked. "Sorting by education, age, and sex."

Jewell smiled at the camera and winked at them. "That's my protégé."

"Found him," Ethan said, and a screen filled with an image and a Washington State driver's license. "Give me another minute, and I'll have his address."

"I have that." Jewell chuckled when Ethan cussed. "He's in Switzerland." She cocked her head.

"He's been there for five years. Are you sure we have the right guy?"

"Did he work for Plume?"

"He still does," Ethan said. "Plume Pharma based out of Switzerland."

Jacob looked at Joseph. Shit was not as it seemed. "Who owns Plume?"

"I'm on it," Jewell said. Ethan's fingers flew over the keyboard. "Looks like he transferred there five years ago. He lives in a company-owned house. His financials are coming up on the screen." She paused. "Okay, this one will take a hot minute. So far, I have three empty levels of shell companies. Ethan, feel like a challenge?"

"I'm on it. Send it my way." The man cracked his fingers and said, "Come to Poppa."

"You better not be a poppa, or your dad will have your head." Fury chuckled.

Ethan snorted. "First, I'm over twenty-one, so my parental status isn't his concern any longer. Plus, I'm a dog dad, so deal with it, Uncle Joseph."

Joseph growled something under his breath about Ethan being a smartass, and the wolf sat up. His ears pinned forward, and his eyes fixed on Joseph.

Jacob laughed at his brother. "I don't think Thor likes your growling."

His brother slid his gaze from the dog to him. "I don't care."

Jacob would have teased his brother more, but Jason's image appeared on the screen. "Fill me in." Jacob and Joseph told him about the information they'd received from Dr. Montrose. "Who owns Plume?" Jason demanded.

"Right now, a conglomerate of nothing," Ethan said. "I'm digging."

"Do we have eyes on Dion Francis?" Jason asked.

"Nope. I don't have any cameras in the residential area that I can tap into … which is hella strange, Jace," Jewell said. "With Bluetooth cameras nowadays, there's always somewhere I can slip into, but not here." She typed faster. "Not within five blocks. Ethan, hold on that search, please, and help me determine who owns this housing block."

"That's easy. Plume Pharma," Ethan said. "Check the records I just sent you."

"Okay. Great work, dude. Jace, they own everything within five blocks of the office buildings where they're located. No cameras. Not even street cameras owned by the city."

Jacob asked, "Which city?"

"Basel," Ethan said. "It borders Germany and France."

"Jewell, I need you to contact our people in the scientific community and get us the brightest brains on viruses. They'll be the ones who are going to Plume in Washington State. Find out who's the puppet master of this company. I want to know who's pulling the strings, funding this operation, and potentially profiting from this virus."

"Dr. Montrose knows some people she thinks can help." Jacob didn't want her offer to help not to be forwarded.

"Tell her we appreciate it, and we'll take her up on it should we need to do so, but I want to use our vetted personnel first." Jason took off his glasses and leaned back. "Have we validated the target?"

"Not yet, no," Joseph said. "The question I have is what good would it do to eliminate the Secretary of State?"

"It's a powerful office," Jacob said, although he didn't have a clue who would benefit from that particular demise. "So who would gain the most in that situation?"

"Probably whoever steps up into the position," Ethan said as he typed.

Jacob looked at his brother on the screen. "It is a political appointment."

Ethan turned around. "Not just that office. Everyone moves up, right? Some of those offices are pretty powerful, too. It might not be the top layer."

Jacob blinked and did a double take at the man who was just yesterday a child. Where had time gone?

"Ethan, you're brilliant," Jewell said. "We can get those likely moves, Jace. It would jiggle a lot of offices, for sure."

"Get me the information, please." Jason nodded. "Good idea, Ethan. Jacob and Joseph, do you need anything from us?"

"Information, and as quickly as possible," Joseph said.

"I'm on it, bubba." Jewell looked up at the camera.

Joseph smiled at his sister. "I know it, Button, but I'm referring to the virus, too. If this threat is validated, Jason may have to advise the president to have us bow out of it."

"I briefed him this morning. The United States

will not be threatened. We need to be seen as a leader in this event. His words, not mine." Jason put his glasses back on.

"Jason, you said we were volunteered for the interior control of the venue. Who was that by?" Jacob asked the question every one of his team members wanted to know.

"It came from the State Department through the president. France knows about the threat, and this relieves them of any responsibility should something go wrong." Jason shook his head. "I have repeatedly requested the French authorities be allowed to work alongside us, but that idea has been shot down each time."

"Do we know who in the State Department?" Joseph asked.

"No. I haven't been able to find that out."

"I can," Jewell said. "I can get that."

Jason smiled at her. "Legally?"

"Okay, no … So … Wait! Con can get that. He has contacts he can leverage," Jewell revised her answer, and Jacob hid a smile. His sister was the best at what she did. Legal or not.

"Bring him in on it and let him work his magic," Jason said.

"Magic, my ass," Joseph grumbled.

"What was that about your ass?" Jason lifted his eyebrows. "I thought you and Con had reconciled your differences." Joseph snorted and crossed his arms over his chest. Jason sighed and shook his head. "That's what I thought. Oh, and say hi to Mom for me tonight, will you? Archangel out."

Jason's picture went dark.

"Asshole," Joseph growled.

"I can still hear you," Jason's voice came over the monitor's speaker.

"Oh, sorry." Jewell hit a few keys. "Okay, he's gone."

Joseph rolled his eyes and sat up to lean on the table with his elbows. "So, we need to know who owns Plume, why this Francis dick is still working for them, why there are no cameras around Plume in Switzerland, and then locate the fucker, so we can watch or possibly question him."

"We can talk to Anubis and get one of the baby class to head that way. But we don't want an international incident, so monitor until we have something solid to go forward with."

"Send two babies," Joseph said as he stood up. "We need twenty-four-hour coverage on this guy."

Jacob nodded. "I agree. Let's head over there and then go say hi to the 'rents."

"What time is it?" Joseph said, glancing around the computer room.

"Fifteen hundred hours," Ethan said, then changed his voice. "Dinner is at six, boy. Don't be late."

Joseph laughed. "You sound like Frank."

"Thanks!" Ethan said and continued to type. "I'll take that compliment all day."

CHAPTER 17

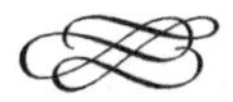

Lillian watched as the small jet landed. "I hope you like him." She held Billy's hand as they waited by the small building that held the radar equipment for the landing strip.

He squeezed her hand. "If he's important to you, he's important to me."

She looked up at him and smiled. "Have I told you today I love you?"

"You have, but I'm not averse to hearing it again." Still holding her hand, he wrapped his arm around her back and pulled her forward.

She laughed, caught by him like she was. Toeing up, she kissed him on the cheek. "I love you."

"Oh, that won't do, ma'am. Not at all." He

wrapped his other arm around her and pulled her into a kiss. Lillian's laughter dissolved. He released her hand, and she wrapped her arms around his neck. The man's kisses melted her in the absolute best possible way. He turned her into a ball of need and want, and he was the only way to ease those desires.

The sharp whine of the jet's engine as it pulled up next to them on the tarmac separated them. No sooner was the engine off than the door opened. Abe jogged down the stairs and over to her. His dark skin and close-cropped black hair were a sight for sore eyes, but that smile … his smile was the smile of her best friend. He picked her up and swung her around like his brother Cash had.

"Damn, girl, it's been forever."

"It hasn't been that long." She laughed and patted his chest when he set her down. "I want you to meet someone. Abe, this is Billy Pearson. He and I are …" She stopped and smiled at Billy while extending her hand to him. "We're together."

Billy took her hand and extended his other to Abe. "I've met your brother and worked with him several years ago. It's a pleasure to meet you."

Abe took his hand with a shocked expression.

"Together, you mean, like, together?" The man blinked from her to Billy.

"Abe, I don't know how else to explain it?" She looked at Billy. "Dating isn't enough."

"Definitely not enough." Billy laughed before turning his attention to Abe. "Did you have a good honeymoon? You went to Bali, right?"

"Ah, yeah. Yeah, it was awesome." Abe jerked his head back toward the plane. "I need to go get my bags. I'll be right back."

"Well, he took that well." Billy rolled his eyes but laughed when she poked him in the ribs.

"Stop." Lillian knew Abe would have questions. "I'm going to take him to his room and bring him up to speed. I'll meet you back at your apartment before we head over to Isaac and Lyric's."

"If he gives you any problems, let me know." Billy dropped another kiss on her lips before he winked and walked away.

She turned and waited for Abe to come back. "Where did dude go?"

"Dude? His name is Billy. Give me that." She took his backpack and let him carry his suitcase. There was no way it would roll over the gravel.

"What the hell did he do? Knock on your door the second you got here? I mean, hello, it's only been ... what ... just a couple of months?" Abe jacked his suitcase up over his shoulder.

Lillian stopped and turned to him. "First and foremost, I love you like a brother, and as a sister to a brother ... *don't*. Don't try to belittle what I have here. It's good, and it's healthy, and I love the man."

"Wow. Now it's love?" Abe dropped the suitcase to the ground. "Do you think maybe you should go talk to someone?" Lillian dropped his backpack on the ground. "Hey, my computer's in there."

She glanced down at the backpack. "Tough shit, you won't need it here anyway." She narrowed her eyes at her teammate. "Abe Costello, you fell in love with Heather over the course of a weekend. *Two days*. Two. Count them. One and two." She lifted a finger with each word and then wiggled them at him. "Do not pull this high and mighty routine with me. You can either be happy for me and get to know one of the best men I've ever met, or you can never talk about him or me with him again. Those are the only two options you have. Period, end of sentence. Full stop. No more. Do you copy?"

He put his hands on his hips and stared at her.

"Well, at least he isn't that guy who made you feel like shit when you first got here."

Lillian rolled her eyes and picked up Abe's backpack. She'd never admit to Abe it was Billy. That would be her secret for the rest of her life. "We have a lot of information to go over."

"Hey, Lil, wait up." He hefted the suitcase over his shoulder and fell into step with her. "I'm happy for you. Just shocked. You got to admit, I had no warning."

"Then, behave yourself." She threw him a narrowed glance.

He held up his hand. "Scouts honor."

"Good. We do have a lot of information to go over." She looked around. There was no one around them. "Dion may be working on Tarmilse. It could be the agent we need to protect our Guardians against."

Abe stopped. "Dion the Dick? That can't happen. The study was vaulted."

She turned to him. "Yeah, about that … Come on, we shouldn't talk here."

"Wait, how do you know this?"

"I'll fill you in, but we need to be in a secure area." She looked at him and widened her eyes. "Sometime today, Costello."

He jerked and started walking. "Holy hell, I've missed a lot, haven't I?"

"Yeah. Cash is waiting at the barracks for us. He'll get you settled, and then we'll go to the classroom, which is secure, and I'll bring you up to speed by the numbers."

Abe stopped again. "Look at all the cows."

She stopped and turned to look at the pastures. "They've already moved some. There used to be more over that way."

He pointed. "Horses. Man, do you think we'll get a chance to ride?"

Lillian laughed. "I'll ask Billy. He'll know how to make that happen."

Abe turned to look at her. "Well, then, he's now officially my best friend. You're out."

She laughed and pulled his shirt. "Come on, cowboy. We've got work to do."

"Always the spoilsport."

"Someone has to be." She'd just got him started toward the barracks when Cash came flying out of the building. Abe dropped his suitcase, and the brothers collided. Lillian watched the back thumping and listened to the muffled greetings as they hugged each other.

"Dude, Lil has a man."

Cash picked up the suitcase, and Abe grabbed his backpack. "I was just informed."

"He's a smartass, but he's a damn good man. One of the best snipers on the planet, too, and your overwatch for this mission, so once again, you've lucked the fuck out." Cash hit his brother with a punch to the arm. "That's for not telling me I had to give a toast at your wedding."

"You were the fucking best man, Cash. Haven't you been to weddings before?" Abe said as they walked to the building Cash had flown out of minutes earlier.

"Well, yeah, but I didn't know it was a thing, okay? I've never been a best man before. All my team is single, thank God."

"That will change eventually." Lillian laughed.

"Nope. We're diehard bachelors," Cash said. "Wrench, Pops, Cowboy, Ace, and I have taken the oath. Never going to happen."

Lillian laughed so hard her stomach hurt. "You realize you just sealed your own fate, right?"

"Never going to happen, woman. Now, let me settle him, then I'll bring him to the classroom."

"Deal." Lillian hugged them, then headed to the classroom to set up for Abe's crash catch-up course.

* * *

SHE LEANED BACK and stretched her back. “So, the protocols have been streamlined.”

“That makes sense.” Abe took the papers and read her notes. They’d worked together for so long that he was one of the few who could make sense out of her handwriting. The fables about the horrible doctor’s handwriting were true in her case. She didn’t have pretty, legible cursive. It was hit-and-miss if she could read it sometimes.

There was a knock at the door, and they both turned to look. She smiled widely as Billy walked in and said, “We have a party to go to in about an hour. I figured you’d want to shower and decompress before we left.”

“Oh, that would be good.” Lillian stood and stretched.

“How did the fast-pass go?” Billy asked as he came over and put his arm around her.

“He’s my best student.” Lillian put her hand on Abe’s shoulder.

“Dude, Lil said you might be able to hook me up with a ride on a horse.”

Billy blinked. “Sure, not a problem. Do you ride?”

"No, but I've always wanted to. We lived next to this old crappy ass pasture, and there was this horse that lived in it. I was always over there. I loved that old thing. But one day, I came home from school, and it was gone. The owner sold it for slaughter. Man, I cried for a week, and I'm not embarrassed to say it, either." Abe lifted his chin and stared at Billy, almost daring him to say anything about crying.

"Horses are amazing. They can sense a person's soul, or so I've been told. I believe it. Do you know where the owner is now? We could go have a word with him."

Abe snorted out a laugh. "Her, and no, but, man, I'm on board with that visit. If I ever find out, I'll let you know."

"Deal." Billy extended his hand, and Abe shook it.

"You two get out of here. I'm going to go over these notes again, and then I'll wander back to the barracks. Cash was talking about going to the Bit and Spur for a couple drinks."

"It's a nice little bar," Lillian said, and Abe whipped his head up.

"You went to a bar?"

"What? I can't go to a bar?" She put her hand on her hip.

"You've never wanted to go with Heather and me," Abe said.

Billy laughed. "Put it together, Abe."

The man frowned and gave Lillian a frustrated look. "Because Heather is jealous of you."

"Bingo." Lillian laughed. "If you ask me to go here, I'll check with my man and see if we can make it."

Abe shook his head. "I keep telling her she has no reason to be jealous."

"She has every reason. Well, had," Billy said as he stared down at her. "She's taken now."

Abe clapped his hands. "Yes, hallelujah. Maybe that will stop her craziness about Lil."

Billy threw back his head and laughed. "Lillian is an exceptionally beautiful woman. Good luck with that, my friend." Lillian stared up at Billy as he spoke directly to her and not to Abe.

"Oh, barf and gag. Please don't tell me Heather and I are this mushy."

"Worse." Lillian didn't bother to look at her friend.

"Fine. I'll look at the notes tomorrow. I'm out of here."

"Bye," she said as she heard him go.

"I thought he'd never leave." Billy dropped for a kiss.

Lillian sighed and curled into the big, hard body she knew almost better than her own.

"Let's get you downstairs and into decompression mode." Billy picked up her notes for her and dropped his arm around her shoulders. She'd never felt so cherished. But her therapist had told her she would find someone who would treat her as if she was worthy of respect, and they would honor the boundaries she set. Who knew she'd have to travel to the middle of nowhere to find him?

CHAPTER 18

Billy watched from the tower as the teams moved into the mock venue. They were on the fourth scenario of the afternoon. It was just as important for him to know how the teams would deploy as it was for them to know where he and the other marksmen were located. The medical teams would be onsite tomorrow. As they rapidly approached their deployment, they were working together more. His phone vibrated in his pocket, but he ignored it until the scenario was over. He pulled it out when "Knock it off" was called, and the teams lowered their weapons.

He pushed redial. "What's up?"

"Are you done for the day?" Mike's voice came over the connection.

"Should be. The teams are going to do a debrief. We normally stick around for it, but I can bolt if you need me."

"Alpha wants you to sit in on a briefing with Dr. Montrose."

"I'll be there. Which conference room?"

"Lower level."

"Give me twenty minutes."

Billy shouldered his weapon. He grabbed the rope attached to the apex of the structure he was in, wrapped his leg, and lowered himself down. Specter met him outside the mock building. "I've been recalled for a meeting. Can you catch a ride in with Asp and Alex?"

"Not a problem." Specter tossed him the keys to the truck they used to get out to the training area.

"Thanks." He jogged to the truck, secured his weapon in its case, and headed back to the annex.

Mike met him in the common area as they both headed to the conference room. "What's wrong?"

"Nothing that I know of. Alpha asked for both of you, so I jumped." Mike chuckled. "That's what happens when your old team leader is onsite."

"That's right. You were on the original Alpha Team."

"Crazy times," Mike said. "We blazed some

trails and cheated death more times than we should have."

He seriously understood that. "Sounds about right."

Lillian was sitting in the conference room when they arrived. She looked up and smiled. "What's the meeting about?"

"I have no idea," Billy said as he sat down beside her.

"Me either. I'm an errand boy today." Mike laughed. He bent backward and looked down the hall they'd just walked down. "Here they come. I'm outta here. Going to go do the job I'm paid to do."

"Bye," Lillian said. She leaned over as soon as he was gone, and Billy kissed her. "How's today going?"

"Pretty good. I think we're ready as far as the teams are concerned. A couple more days working with everyone, and we'll be ready for this mission." He dropped his arm around her shoulders. The bosses knew they were an item, and he sensed she was concerned about the meeting.

"Thanks for coming in," Alpha said as he entered. Fury shut the door behind them. They both sat down across from where he and Lillian were sitting.

"Here's the no-shit facts," Fury started. "We can't find that asshat Francis. Passport control has him in Switzerland. Residential records show him as a tenant of an apartment building owned by Plume Pharma. Employment records show him as an employee of the same company. There are no cameras in the area. Our people on the ground have not seen him."

Lillian leaned forward. "Did you say Plume employed him? Still? That can't be. He was fired." She looked from Fury to Alpha. "That can't be right."

"Our people are certain this branch of Plume is his employer. At least on paper," Alpha restated.

"What did the lab say about the vaulted project?" Lillian grabbed her pen in a death grip. Billy put his hand on her back, causing her to jump a bit.

"They denied any project of that name. They also denied firing asshat." Fury sneered.

Lillian stood up. "That's not true! You can ask Abe. He was there. He knows."

Alpha lifted his hand. "We believe you. Do you still have the photos of his work?"

She deflated and planted in the chair. "No.

They made me clear them from my phone. They watched as I did it."

"Our specialists have scoured through their computer systems, unbeknownst to them. There's no information indicating any of the events you described."

Lillian shook her head. "No, he can't do this to me again. I'm not insane. I know what I saw, what I did. Mrs. Buchanan! She was the board member who pushed for him to be fired."

"She's dead." Fury shook his head. "Died in a freak accident. She fell down a small flight of stairs and broke her neck."

"We firmly believe the company is covering up," Alpha interjected. "The question is, what are they covering up and why?"

"Well, Termilse, for one." Lillian shook her head. "So, there would be no antidote?"

Both Alpha and Fury glanced at each other. Fury nodded, and Alpha leaned forward. "Have you ever heard of a blood-based antidote for any contagion?"

Lillian shook her head. "No. Something like that would rock the medical world. Why?"

Alpha leaned forward. "This is classified at the

highest level. We have in our possession three vials of an antidote that will neutralize any contagion."

Lillian shook her head. "How is that possible?"

Alpha narrowed his eyes. "The logistics are as highly classified as the knowledge that this exists. There isn't a widespread production of this antidote. The person whose blood was used was tortured for most of her life as diseases and viruses were medically introduced into her system."

"That's reprehensible! Human experimentation? Whoever did that to her should be brought up on charges!"

Billy fucking agreed with her, but instead of being brought up on charges, the bastard should be terminated.

"The person responsible is dead. As far as the world is now concerned, she's also dead. We're protecting her. If anyone were to find out about her …"

"The implications would be catastrophic." Lillian planted both hands on the table and seemed to focus between them. "If the wrong people found out …" She lifted her eyes. "The evil in this world can never know she lives. But then again, her blood could be used to solve so many problems.

Both good and bad people would go to extraordinary lengths to use her."

Fury nodded. "Exactly. That's why *you* and *you alone* will be in possession of these three vials. Should by some circumstance this Termilse be injected, ingested, breathed in, or however it is released, your mission will be to inoculate this specific list of personnel."

Alpha pushed a single piece of paper over to her. "The dosage is point two five ml. On the day of the event, you will prepare one vial for possible use. The third vial will be reserved for use at our direction. Your comms and Billy's will have an extra channel. Billy, you are to ensure no one stops her."

Billy tapped the list in front of Lillian. "This list doesn't have any Guardians on it. How can she safely give the shots if she's sick or dying?"

"She won't be sick. None of you will be."

"Because we are inoculating everyone prior to departure," Lillian said. "With that dosage, we can protect everyone and the people listed here."

"Exactly. There's so much more going on than what you've been allowed to know. This situation has a global impact on the peace accord, but we believe something else is happening. I'm not at liberty to discuss it." Alpha pinned them both with a hard stare. "No one can know of this. Call it a booster shot or whatever you think the medical personnel will believe. You'll need to give the shots tomorrow."

"To give it the most time in our system." She nodded. "I'll handle it."

"The teams will line up and bare their arms. They know the drill," Fury said.

Billy leaned forward. "Sir, this antidote is safe, right?"

Alpha chuckled. "It's safe. You'll never get a cold again."

Lillian looked at him. "Or cancer?"

Alpha shrugged. "I haven't seen the research. I don't know the answer to that."

"Sir, you said global implications besides the actual peace treaty. Where's the threat coming from?"

Alpha shook his head. "We're still tracking that down. Whoever's playing the game has plenty of resources, but our team is on the trail. They're the best at this type of investigation. Again, I can't stress enough that the information I've given you is classified at the highest levels. *No one* can know."

"Yes, sir," Lillian said as Billy nodded his understanding.

Fury reached into the pocket of his utility uniform and retrieved a small, hard-sided black case. "It doesn't need to be refrigerated unless it's over eighty degrees Fahrenheit."

Lillian took the case from him. She looked up at Alpha and Fury. "May I?"

They nodded. She opened the case, and Billy peeked in. "It's not red."

Lillian laughed. "No, it wouldn't be." She glanced back at the bosses. "I'll protect it with my life."

"And I'll protect her life with mine." Billy put his hand on her back.

She glanced over at him and smiled. "I know you will."

"Then we're done here." Fury stood up.

"Sir, could I ask a favor?" Lillian stopped the men.

"You can ask. I can't guarantee we'll be able to say yes."

"When you find out what's going on at Plume, make them pay the piper? That type of unethical work shouldn't be allowed."

Fury's smile was wide and wicked. "Oh, that's a promise I will gladly make and keep."

CHAPTER 19

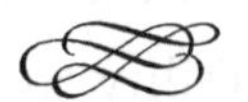

Billy woke suddenly. He listened for anything that could have woken him up and then glanced at the clock. "Did I wake you?" Lillian said from beside him.

"Maybe. Something did," he admitted. "Why are you awake?" He rolled over to face her.

"I don't know." She moved closer to him and snuggled against his chest.

He wrapped her in his arms. "Are you worried about the deployment?"

She shook her head. "No, not really. We've practiced, and everyone knows what to do."

"Is it Dion the Dick?"

She chuckled. "It's a catchy name, isn't it?"

"It is. I kinda like saying it." He yawned and settled his chin on the top of her head.

"I think the information they gave us today is what's making me so upset. I couldn't imagine what that woman went through. And the implications of her blood's ability to do what it does. My mind is blown, and yet, I can't say anything because it isn't fair to her ... but is it fair to those who are dying?" She sighed. "It's a moral dilemma."

"No, it isn't." He flicked the thin blanket over them. "You can't tell anyone. There's no dilemma for you or me. You're bound by your security classification, and you saying anything would land you and me in jail."

She tipped back to look at him. "How would it land you in jail?"

Billy made a pfft noise, then yawned again. "Like I'd let you go anywhere without me."

She laughed. "It is cut and dried, isn't it." She slid her arm over his waist and sighed. "I'm building a mountain where there isn't even a molehill."

Billy chuckled and arched his hips into her. "A little more than a molehill, but not quite a mountain yet."

Lillian laughed as he dropped and rolled her on

top of him. "Are you asking me if I want to go mountain climbing, sir?"

"Is that code for what I think you're thinking? If so, yes."

"I can try to scale to the summit, but you usually help me over the ridge." She sat up and ground down onto his cock.

"Don't tease me, woman," Billy growled and lifted his hips.

"Who said I was teasing?" She lifted a bit and reached under her, taking his now very hard cock in hand and guiding him to her center. She slowly lowered. The sensation of taking him that way was so different, yet so familiar. She lifted and braced her hands on his shoulders and then lowered again. His hands cupped her breasts and rolled her nipples as she rocked back and forth.

She lost her rhythm and moved her hips when he was deep inside her. The sound the man made was feral and filled with need. Lillian lifted, lowered, and moved against him again. His hands grabbed at the bedding, and he tightened his arms, popping all the muscles of his chest and neck. She watched as she did it again. He grabbed her arms, lifted, and flipped their positions without separating them.

His pace was fast and hard. Her body responded, and as he chased his release, he once again pushed her to that beautiful oblivion where her body rippled in heavenly sensation. He roared as he crashed through his climax and then dropped down to her. She held him against her, not caring that breathing was difficult. He had become her world, and she'd hold onto him as long as she lived.

* * *

BILLY HEFTED his pack onto his back and slipped his arms through the straps. He picked up his rifle and grabbed Lillian's pack. "I can get it," she said as she checked her medical kit again.

"You take care of that. It's the priority now." Billy waited for her to zip the case.

"You're right."

Billy smiled. "I know."

"Oh, you." Lillian rolled her eyes but walked up to him and toed up so she could kiss him.

"Ready?"

"As I'll ever be." She nodded, and they walked out of the clinic and headed toward the flight line, where a waiting C-17 was parked.

"Do you have your comms?"

"In my pocket," she acknowledged. "Comms made it on the checklist last night after we were issued them."

"Sorry, I don't mean to second-guess you." She had a magnificent mind, and he was probably stepping all over her toes.

"No worries, that's for sure." She smiled up at him. "I'm sure we'll forget something. I just don't want it to be something important."

"You know we won't be able to stay together tonight." He figured he'd be rooming with Specter.

"I know. This morning was pretty amazing, though." She nudged him as they walked to the flight line.

"Just pretty amazing?" He staggered. "I'm ruined."

"You're insane." She laughed and grabbed his arm.

He turned around and walked backward while talking to her. "True, but you knew this about me."

"I did. The first time you willingly talked to me, you told me you had some mental issues." She laughed when he almost fell on his ass.

He spun back around. "Which I've overcome spectacularly, I'll have you know."

Lillian put her arm through his. "Which is why I love you as much as I do."

He looked down at her. "I love you. You are so much more than I deserve."

"And yet, you deserve so much more than I am." She stopped, and so did he. "I don't know what the next forty-eight hours will bring, but no matter what, you have been the most amazing time of my life."

"And you have been the best thing I've ever experienced." He bent down to kiss her, and she put her hand on his chest.

Once they parted, she asked, "When we're done with this mission, could we talk about what comes next?"

Billy smiled down at her. "Absolutely. That's my favorite topic."

Lillian narrowed her eyes at him. "I thought food was your favorite topic."

"Food is second. That's how important you are to me."

In her horrible British accent, Lillian gasped slightly and said, "Then, sir, I'm enshrined in haughty company."

If only she knew how highly he valued her. He'd tried to show her in deed and with his words, but he doubted he'd ever be able to communicate the depth of his love for her. He winked at her and answered, "Indeed, you are, ma'am. Indeed, you are."

He smiled as Lillian joined the medics and went over their checklist with everyone. Specter and he did a rundown of all the equipment. Asp and Alex had gone to France two days ago with their wives. They had all four weapons, enough ammo to start a medium-sized war, and all four packs. The teams filed in first, then the medics, and they were last. Lillian had saved him a jump seat beside her, and Specter volunteered to make sure the rifles and packs were secured, so he made his way to the seat.

He handed her earplugs and then passed them out to the medics. "We need these?" one of the docs asked.

"Oh, yeah." He nodded. "You'll thank me later." He settled in the jump seat and helped Lillian strap in. She grabbed his hand when the thrust of the engine sent them into the air. The trip was bare bones. There was no inflight service, no beds, no flight attendants. The crew chief passed out box meals, and trips to the head were the only time the seat belts came off. Lillian slept on his shoulder, and he dropped his head on top of hers to catch some shuteye.

By the time they landed, every last one of them was in a sour mood. Billy retrieved his and Asp's gear after making sure Lillian was set. Spector had Alex's equipment. He and Specter followed the teams off the plane. The medics were ushered off and into waiting SUVs. They took off ahead of the teams and weapons. Billy hated not being with her, but he had to go through the French agency's briefings on the use of force. Like he cared … but they would play nice. For now.

They converged on the hotel Guardian had rented out for them. It wasn't anything special, but it was secure, and they'd use it for one night. Tonight. Before the sun was up tomorrow morning, they'd deploy to the venue, do their inspections, and take their places. All the practice, all the assumptions, all the preparation would either be for naught, or shit would hit the fan.

Billy hefted the equipment he was responsible for out of the back of the vehicle he'd rode in on the way to the hotel. He was praying for a nice, long, boring-ass day tomorrow.

He took the key he was offered and made his way up the stairwell to the second floor. The room was sufficient, and he was right, Specter was assigned to the room with him.

"I want to go look at the venue tonight," Specter said by way of greeting.

"Wouldn't hurt. Do you need company?" Billy put down his and Asp's gear.

"A couple of my teammates are here. I'm going to meet up with them and get the latest. I'll be back in a few hours."

Billy got it. He didn't need to know Specter's teammates. He nodded. "See you then."

He dropped into one of the full-sized beds and closed his eyes. He hated flying in transports. The seats sucked, but they were the best way to move teams. Twisting, he popped his back, then sat up.

He took out his weapon and meticulously inspected it. It was his entire reason for being there. He was Lillian and Abe's overwatch. The team were rovers, so he was high up in the dome. He was wrapped tight with the added pressure of ensuring Lillian made it to the personnel on that list. Inspecting his weapon loosened some of those muscles as he followed his routine. He unpacked his ruck and carefully placed everything back, ensuring he could access what he needed when he needed it.

By the time he'd finished, Specter was back. "Anything good?" Billy asked as he finished securing the ties on his ruck.

"No." Specter sat down on the bed. "I informed Alpha of what I found out. He says he'll run it to the ground and let us know if it's actionable."

"Care to fill me in?"

"Can't," Specter said, lying down on the bed and covering his eyes with his arm. "If I did, I'd have to kill you."

Billy snorted a laugh and got up to turn off the light. He laid down on the bed and closed his eyes. His watch was set, and he and Specter would sleep fully clothed. Hell, everyone in the hotel would be ready to move at a moment's notice. He thought of Lillian as he fell asleep and prayed the mission went smoothly.

CHAPTER 20

Jacob King rubbed his eyes as he waited for his brother to come online. "I'm here." Jason's growl made him look up.

"CCS found who owns Plume," Jacob said.

"It better be good to drag my ass away from my wife and kids."

Jacob glanced over at his brother Joseph before nodding. "It is. Abrasha Molchalin."

Jason was quiet for a moment. "What else?"

"How did you know there was something else?" Joseph asked, his voice rang with a tinge of humor.

Jason leaned back in his chair. "You two never disappoint."

"Plume Pharma doesn't produce or export. Nor

have they filed for any regulatory advancements for drugs they've patented for the past six years. That is about the same time Molchalin appears to have purchased all the open traded stock for Plume through a maze of shell companies." Jacob explained the information Jewell, Ethan, Honor, and Con had uncovered.

"All right, so what? He's holding a defunct or soon-to-be defunct company. Why does that matter?"

"The time corresponds with the coding of one Benjamin Wellington." Fury dropped that bomb.

Jason leaned forward. "Shit. Was Molchalin one of the entities that raided the bastard's vaults looking for Eve?"

Fury snarled. "I'd lay odds on it. One of the baby class gained access to Plume Pharma."

"Who?" Jason narrowed his eyes.

"Phantom." Fury smiled. "No one saw him."

"He takes risks." Jason growled the words.

Joseph laughed. "He's damn good. He'd just left the facility when he met up with Specter and relayed what he saw. Specter brought it to us. Everyone in the building above the ground floor is wearing personal protective gear. There are airlocks, and the ventilation system is set up to contain any possible spills. He said it was the most intricate he'd ever seen."

"And yet they aren't producing anything." Jason rubbed his chin. "At least nothing legal."

"Which is why we're betting on the connection Ethan and Jewell found. It's a long shot, but the Ambassador from Zaharaania has been diagnosed with stage three pancreatic cancer. He travels with his personal physician."

Jason narrowed his gaze and cocked his head slightly as he stared at them. "I'm waiting ..."

"The doctor who is his personal physician was employed with Plume Pharma until he left their employ to work full time for the ambassador."

"Do we have the name of this doctor?"

"We do, and we've run it. There's no connection to anyone we can place, but that's the way into the event if Molchalin is behind the rumored biochemical threat," Jacob explained. "We need to focus on this contingent as a possible threat."

Jason drew a deep breath and stared off to the side for a long moment. "So, breaking this down by the numbers. Molchalin, a Russian oligarch who recently funded the attempted takeover of Swiss banks by Russian extremists, owns a Swiss business that doesn't seem to do what it's registered to do. Additionally, a medical doctor who once worked for Plume, the same company owned by Molchalin, is now the personal doctor for one of the main participants of this peace accord. We believe Molchalin has the capability to produce the bio-chem component we've been hearing rumors of and believe he's doing this in Switzerland."

Jacob and Joseph said, "Correct," at the same time.

Jason steepled his fingers together. "What does Molchalin stand to gain from this summit not happening or our Secretary of State being killed?"

"Payback, sweet fucking revenge," Joseph said, leaning forward. "It isn't difficult to point the finger at Guardian for defusing Rostova's power play. If Guardian is on the inside controlling the security for an international event while in a foreign country, and shit hits the fan? It would cause ripples through our business and national security. POTUS would think more than twice before using us again. The alphabets would stop cooperation, not wanting to be involved with us. Everyone is saving their own ass and busy protecting what little reputation they have left, and boom, we are persona non grata. Molchalin gets a little of his back."

Jason nodded, then asked, "How could Molchalin influence the Secretary of State's suggestion we assume security in a foreign country to POTUS and the French government's acceptance of the suggestion?"

"Oh, oh, pick me! I know the answer to that one. What is massive lobbyist money and or influence for two thousand, Alex?" Jewell said, and Jacob flicked his eyes to the corner of the screen where her picture appeared. "Molchalin has his many fingers in big Pharma. Not just Plume. We found that out when we were working on Plume's puzzle. Con is running lobbyist donations from his pharma corporations for both the US and France's political parties, super PACs, or individual candidates."

"Bribed," Joseph spat in disgust before he shook his head. "That doesn't surprise me."

"But wait, Jace. There's more. Con just forwarded that report you were looking for on the moves that would happen should the Secretary of State be, ah … well, removed from office." Jewell interrupted the conversation. "It's in your inbox. Jacob and Joseph, you have it, too." Jewell tapped the screen, and everyone looked back at the monitors. "Recognize any of those names?" The names appeared on the screen. There were five highlighted in red.

"I do," Jason said and swore bitterly. "Is there any connection between any person on this list and Molchalin, big pharma, or either of the factions involved in the treaty?"

"Hold on. Con's online with me, and we're running it."

Jacob's eyes never left his brother Jason's face. He'd seen that hard look before. "What are you thinking, Jace?"

"We've been maneuvered into a box, and I have a sneaking suspicion I know who's moving the players and now who's paying for movement. I just don't know why it's being done." A vicious smile spread across his face. "Fortunately, we have the best fucking people in the world working for us. I need to make some calls. Jewell, send me that information as soon as you have it."

"You got it," she said without looking up at the camera.

"And our people in France?" Jacob queried.

Jason looked up at the camera. "Are protected. Get ahold of the team leaders and our overwatches. Get pictures of the ambassador, his vehicles, his doctor, security, and everything we can on who he's bringing with him. Passports will have been scanned, but that doesn't mean last-minute additions can't happen. But caution them: Molchalin isn't our only threat."

"We've driven that into them for the last month. They're ready, Jason. We hand-picked the best."

"Then brief them on the new intel and let them do their jobs. Archangel out."

Jacob turned his attention. "Jewell, we'll need a video feed to France."

Jewell stopped typing for a moment. "Now? Aren't they sleeping?"

"No. I doubt anyone slept last night, but they're moving into positions shortly, so please set it up and send every scrap of information you have on the ambassador's entourage to the team leaders and overwatches."

"You got it. Hold, please." Her picture disappeared, and he looked over at Joseph.

"Ever wish you were still in the field?" Jacob sat back in his chair.

"Yes. Every time I talk to one of the infants working out there now."

"Infants? They're capable and damn good at what they do."

Joseph slowly rolled his head toward Jacob. "We were better."

"We were. But I'm glad it's them out there instead of me. I've sown my wild oats."

"Being behind a desk makes me itch." Joseph sighed.

"Everything makes you itch." Jacob laughed. "All bullshit aside, the ones we have working for us now are damn good. Well, at least my teams." He had to poke the junkyard dog in his brother.

"The assassins are quality," Joseph mumbled.

"Oh, damn, that had to hurt." Jacob laughed.

"The assassins are. Our computer people need help."

Jacob laughed harder. "Don't start, brother. Don't do it. You will regret it."

"I know you're not talking about me," Jewell said from the blank screen.

"Never, Button. Others, maybe."

"You realize he can hear everything I can hear, right?"

"Yeah, and he's not going to do anything either." Jacob laughed. "Con and Joey have been firmly put in their separate corners."

"France coming online in five …" Jewell's words sobered Jacob immediately. When the screen activated, he looked at his three team leaders and Asp.

"The other overwatches?" Jacob asked.

"Behind the screen. Not enough room." Asp lifted his chin in the direction of the other men.

"All right. We have new information to brief you on. CCS, has the supplemental documentation been sent to them?"

Jewell's voice came over the connection, loud and clear. "Roger that."

"Check your email and make sure your teams get this information, too, but make sure you're in a secure location when you brief them." Jacob went on to explain the suspected connection with the Ambassador of Zaharaania.

"Are there any questions?"

"The French are processing the vehicles into the area. Are they aware of this information?"

"No. Not that I'm aware, nor do I believe they'll be told. At this point, we have the interior, and it's up to us to keep the ambassadors of both countries and the rest of the political representatives safe."

Cash raised his hand. "Alpha, should we put one of our teams on the gate and inspect the cars?"

Jacob shook his head. "No. We do this the way we planned it. The French contingent will ensure the people in the cars have the proper documentation and the vehicles are swept. Your response positions inside the venue need to be manned. Should we have an issue, or the snipers see something, the team in that sector will respond, by the numbers, as we trained."

"You want us to have eyes on the participants as they exit the vehicles." Asp nodded and looked over at the camera toward where Jacob assumed the others were standing.

"Damn straight," Joseph growled. "Four scopes on each vehicle unless there's a situation, then you're on the medics."

"Copy that."

"From the car to the door of the building, too," Jacob added. "Charlie Team, let me know when you're satisfied with your setup in the conference area."

"Roger that, Skipper," Charlie Team leader acknowledged.

"Does anyone have any questions?"

"Yes, sir. Do we have a green light if we see something go sideways?" That was Billy.

Jacob looked at Joseph before nodding. "Do what you need to do. We'll fly high cover. Just get those assholes to sign that document."

There was a rumble of laughter from France. "Do whatever it takes," Jacob said in way of closing.

"As long as it takes." The rumble came back in unison, and the screen went dark.

"I'm grabbing a short nap, then heading to Ethan's office. I want to watch this via satellite coverage." Jacob stood up.

"Sounds like a plan," his brother agreed. "This is the part of missions I hate. Waiting sucks."

"Hopefully, we'll be bored to death today," Jacob spoke as they left the conference room.

Joseph shook his head. "There will be death, but my gut is telling me it won't be from boredom."

CHAPTER 21

Lillian's heart raced. The grandeur and history of the buildings surrounding her were shocking. Almost as shocking as the machine gun armed guards at several checkpoints along the route to the venue. The teams and the overwatches left before the medics, which was as they'd planned, but that meant she wouldn't see Billy. He would already be at perch high above the ground. She leaned back and looked up at the dome.

"Looking for someone?" Lillian gasped and jumped at Billy's question.

"You." She laughed. "Why aren't you up there?" She motioned toward the building.

"I needed to talk to you. Where's Abe?" Billy turned to search the area.

She tapped Billy on the arm when she found her teammate. "Right over there."

"Let's go." Billy moved quickly.

"What's wrong?" Lillian almost had to run to keep up with him.

"Nothing. Just new intelligence."

Billy motioned to Abe, and the man came over. "I thought you'd be up—"

"Not yet," Billy interrupted. "We have new intelligence. The ambassador from Zaharaania has stage three cancer. His doctor worked for Plume Pharma before taking the job as a personal physician. The ambassador travels with his physician, full time."

"That's odd," Abe said, frowning. "Not traveling with your medic, if you have the money, good on you, but the connection is pretty damning."

"It is in more ways than I have time to brief you on," Billy acknowledged. "The way we see it, if there's a way in for the threat we've been preparing for, it's through that doctor. But we can't negate other avenues. I want you two to be on the lookout for anything unusual. You're the roaming team, but unless you're needed, I need you stationary. Stay together. I mean that. Don't get separated; if you see anything that seems odd, you're immediately on the comms. Copy?"

Lillian nodded. "Is there any area you want us to concentrate on being in?"

Billy's eyes narrowed. "Stay in the front entrance area, but I want you back by the stone fence over there. There's an abutment you can stand behind, which will protect you from any explosion."

"Bombs. Oh, goodie. I almost forgot about that possibility." Abe rubbed his neck. "The other teams are hunkering down in their sectors. We've got this area. It isn't a hundred yards to the drive. We'll be able to respond. Yeah. I think you're right."

"I do, too. If we're on the other side of the drive, cars, personal security, or God forbid, debris could keep us from responding in this direction, and that's where the other teams are," Lillian agreed.

"Gather your supplies and head over to that corner. I have to get in position." After dropping a quick kiss on her lips, he was gone.

"He's a good man," Abe said as they returned to where they'd left their kits.

Left breathless, Lillian nodded. “He is. The packs are by the van.”

“The van moved.” Abe swung his head around. “Over there.” He pointed to where their bags were sitting. When they got to them, she and Abe took a quick inventory. It didn’t look like anything had been disturbed. She swung her pack on her back and waited for Abe to finish his inspection. “Damn it, Lil. I’m not sure I signed up for this when we signed that contract with Guardian.”

“We probably didn’t, but if we don’t do this, who will? How many could die?” Lillian patted the vials she had in the padded container in her utility pants. She’d kept them with her since she’d been given them, and the feel of them was comforting.

“Stop making sense when I’m complaining, Lil.” Abe stood up and shouldered his pack.

Lillian chuckled as they walked along the drive. “Dignitaries are arriving.” The voice in her ear momentarily scared her. She grabbed her chest.

“Whoa, I totally forgot about the comms.”

“Me, too. Let’s hustle out of sight.” Abe started to jog, and she fell in beside him. They’d just made it to the corner when the first long SUV entered the gate. A long black car with flags flying on each side of the hood followed.

Lillian leaned against the wall, her pack still strapped to her back. She watched a steady procession of dignitaries enter and walk up the stairs.

"US Secretary of State is next followed by the Ambassador of Zaharaania," the voice said.

Abe sank into a crouch, and she moved closer to him. The security around the Secretary of State was just as impressive as the other dignitaries. She pulled her eyes away from that gaggle of people in time to see the SUV for the Ambassador of Zaharaania pull forward.

She jolted. "Abe." She pounded on his shoulder. "The SUV. Back seat closest to us. Is that Dion?"

"What?" Abe thrust up. "I can't see."

"Here, move up this way." Lillian jogged toward a tree halfway between the drive and the wall.

"Mercy Team Five, status?"

Abe answered, "Hold on. We might have something."

"Define something." Billy's voice cracked over the comms.

"Dion. I thought I saw Dion," Lillian provided.

"Which vehicle?" Asp asked.

"The black SUV," Lillian said.

"Be more specific." The command from

someone she didn't know whipped over the comms.

"The one pulling up to the steps now." Abe moved past the tree. "The doors are opening."

Lillian stayed at the tree. "Come back here. Damn it, Abe. We aren't supposed to be out here."

Abe waved her off. "Just a minute. I have to make sure."

"Abe!" Lillian hissed.

He stopped when men started getting out of the vehicle. The man she thought was Dion didn't turn their way.

"Is it him?"

"I can't tell," Lillian said.

Abe called, "Yo, Dion."

All the men who'd exited the vehicle turned toward Abe.

Lillian felt her heart jump into her throat as she croaked, "Yes. It's him."

Dion's head swiveled from them to the other direction.

"Charlie Team deploy sector one." Lillian heard the command, but her eyes were fixed on Dion.

"Which one?" Billy said.

"The one in the black suit. From the back seat. Black suit," Lillian said again.

Abe started backpedaling toward the tree. The men moved as one toward Abe. The ambassador turned to see what his people were doing but was hustled into the building by the French dignitaries there to meet him.

Lillian grabbed Abe. "I have the target. Let him walk a few more feet toward you," Billy said. "Almost there."

An explosion from the back of the compound rocked the ground under Lillian's feet. A spray of gunfire pelted the front of the building at the same time.

"Code Red. Code Red. We have civilians and Guardians down."

Lillian swung her attention from Dion to the plume of smoke rising behind the buildings. "We need to go help."

"Foxtrot Team responding."

"This is Mercy Team Four. We need ambulances to respond. Two DOA, at least six down."

"Billy, take the shot." Asp's voice rang out.

"I lost the target." Billy's voice sounded strange.

"Are you hit?" Asp asked.

Lillian stopped in her tracks and looked up at the domed building.

"I'll be all right. Target acquired. Fuck."

Another explosion rocked the back area. Lillian dropped to the ground as another spray of bullets hit the front of the building. "Lil."

Abe's voice turned her. She froze. Dion held a gun on her best friend. He sneered and shot without looking at Abe. She jolted forward, and Dion lurched, grabbing her. He pulled her back into his chest, and that was when she saw the needle he held in his other hand.

"What a glorious day. I killed that fucker, and I'll let you spread the contagion. Your death will be ugly, bitch." He wrapped his arm around her neck and took the cap off the needle with his teeth. He spit the cap out and moved the needle toward her neck.

Lillian could see the dome. She knew Billy was up there, and he was waiting for his shot. She closed her eyes and said, "Dion, look up."

She felt Dion's body move and then the jolt and jerk as they both fell backward. The distinct sound of the marksman's rifle fired several more times. Lillian did not move. She laid still and waited for the comms in her ear to tell her it was okay. But there was no order to move, no all-clear given.

She didn't know how long passed before she heard someone running toward her. "Lillian!" At

Billy's call, she sat up, slipped out of her backpack, and immediately crawled over to Abe. Using his pack, she pulled out gauze pads and held them to the wound in his abdomen. "Fuck," she hissed. "Guardian, I need an ambulance. Medic down."

She reached up to touch the damn comms device and realized it wasn't in her ear. Billy slid down beside her. "Is he alive?"

"Yes, we need an ambulance." Lillian worked like a maniac, using Billy as her assistant until French ambulance drivers loaded him onto a cart. She dropped from her knees to her ass and looked over at Billy.

"You're bleeding." She reached for his shirt.

"I'll be okay. We need to head to the back." Billy grabbed Abe's pack and helped her stand. She looked for her pack and found it. Dion's face was missing, and her pack was on his chest. Lillian bent down. The needle had been embedded in the pack next to where her neck would have been. She carefully lifted the needle from her pack. "I need something to put this in."

"Hold on." Billy lowered the pack and winced but dug through until he found a small plastic sharps container. After he opened the top, she put the syringe inside, and Billy put the small plastic container in the side pocket of his utility pants. "We need to help."

Lillian nodded and grabbed her pack, taking one more look at Dion. Funny, she knew she should feel something, but she didn't.

CHAPTER 22

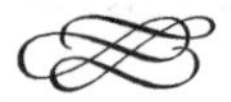

Billy did whatever he was told as Lillian gave clear, concise directions. He saw Asp and Specter assisting the other medics. Alex had taken over the dome and was working with the teams as they continued to provide security for the summit. He'd give the politicians credit, they weren't budging, and they were going to sign that fucking document.

When the last of the injured were loaded into the ambulance, he lifted his utility shirt. Blood from the injury had clotted to the shirt, and the result was fresh blood. "Son of a bitch," he groaned. Lillian was by his side instantly.

"Jesus, Billy," she hissed and rooted around in the pack, looking for supplies.

"It isn't life-threatening." The shots into the dome splintered stone and sent it flying in his direction. He'd pulled several sizable chunks of stone out of the skin on his ribs.

Lillian didn't respond. Instead, she started cleaning the wounds. "You have metal here. Lie down."

"I can wait."

Lillian's eyes snapped up from where she was working. "Damn it, Billy, if you don't lie down, I'm going to knock you on your ass."

Billy blinked at the command. "Are you okay?"

She shook her head. "Not in the slightest. Now, lie down."

"You better do that." He heard Fury's voice in his comms. "Tell her Abe made it to surgery. Our doc at the hospital said things are looking good."

Billy relayed the comment, and she nodded as she took a pair of wicked-looking tweezers and removed the metal embedded under his skin. He lifted a bloody hand and moved her hair from the side of her face. Blood, brain, and skin were still in her hair. "I'm sorry. I should have been there for Abe."

"You were being shot at. None of this was your fault."

In his ear, he heard, "The peace accord has been signed. Dignitaries are leaving. No pomp, no pictures. Charlie and Foxtrot, you're on the front. Echo, you still have the rear."

Billy repeated for her, "They signed the papers."

Lillian looked up at him. "Who did what?"

"The peace accord went through."

She blinked. "Oh, that's good. I'm going to butterfly these together. You need stitches, but …"

Billy waited until she finished and sat up. "Let's gather your teams and get their status."

Lillian nodded, and they stood up. She looked around at the debris from the old stone wall. Lifting her hands, she asked, "How?"

"A kitchen worker. She had a bomb strapped to her chest. The second one was in her purse in the kitchen." Billy walked with her to the rally point. Her medics were gathering.

"How do you know that?" She frowned.

"We've been getting updates," he said and pointed to his ear.

She sighed and looked back toward where he'd dropped Dion. "I lost my comms."

"I know. I thought you were dead." Billy had never felt so afraid in his life. He slammed down those stairs after he'd taken out every last one of those motherfuckers standing around her. Asp covered him as he flew to her, and Alex moved up to take over the dome. "You didn't move."

She stopped walking and looked up at him. "Are you kidding? After as many times as you guys told us to not move during training? I was waiting for someone to tell me I could move, but when I heard you, I figured it was safe."

"Well, you can't argue with that logic," Fury said.

Billy rolled his eyes. "Are you going to listen to our entire conversation?" He pointed to his ear to let Lillian know he was talking to someone.

"Seems to be the best one right now. I need popcorn. It could get good."

Lillian sat down on the ground along with the rest of her team. "Injuries?" she asked.

One of her doctors spoke. "Minor cuts and bruises. Echo team had two down. One was transported to the hospital. The other declined medical aid against our advice. Said he'd live."

Lillian looked at him. "Get him here, please."

Billy nodded and whispered to the pest in his ear, "Fury?"

"I heard. Specter, could you fill in the cordon for the injured Echo team member."

"On my way." Specter appeared out of nowhere and moved past the medics.

"How's Abe?" one of the medics asked.

"In surgery. Prognosis is good," Lillian repeated what Billy had said.

Mercy Team Four's doctor asked, "Who was that guy? The one you and Abe located?"

"A person of interest," Lillian said and shook her head. "We've had run-ins with him before."

"I tagged the deceased. A total of seven. But from what I saw, you won't be having any further run-ins with that guy," the same doctor said.

"What's next?" She looked up at Billy.

"Good question. Fury?"

"Sending transport in as soon as dignitaries are clear. The French government wants a debrief. They can have one from us. You guys are heading home. Straight to the flight line and out of the country."

"As soon as the last dignitaries are gone, we're heading to the airport and going home." Billy gave them the information they needed.

"And our team members who are in the hospital?"

"We have docs in place to take over their care. They'll come home when they can be transported."

Billy repeated Fury's answer, finishing with, "I'm starting to feel like a mockingbird."

Fury made a comment followed by a wicked laugh, and Billy rolled his eyes.

"What did he say?" Lillian asked.

"I am not repeating it." Joseph's laugh was wicked, and it made him smile.

Isaac walked up to the group. "Doc, we're ready. Everyone grab their packs, and we'll be loading for the ride to the transport."

Lillian stood as did the others. He put his arm over her shoulders, and she leaned into him.

"I'm worried about Abe."

"Don't be. Cash will stay with him." He'd heard that chatter earlier when they were working on the injured.

"Heather is going to hate me." They trudged to the front of the compound as a helicopter circled overhead. Billy glanced up. "Guardian, we have a helo in the air over the compound."

"Affirmative. That's the French authorities keeping media out of airspace." Jacob King's voice was in his ear now.

He related the information to Lillian, who sighed and nodded. Billy pulled her in and kissed the top of her head. "Heather probably won't like you no matter what you do, babe." He'd met women like her before. "But this wasn't your fault; it wasn't Abe's." It was *his*; he should have risked the shot before the attack started. No, he couldn't. He didn't have a clear shot, which flew in the face of everything he taught his students.

Lillian bumped into him. "This isn't your fault. You were shot … ish." She wiggled her hand in front of her.

He grunted. "It sure as hell felt like I was shot when my flesh split," he acknowledged. "It slugged me to my knees. Otherwise, Dion never would have had the drop on you or Abe."

"Wait." She stopped. "You know you're carrying a possible plague around in that plastic holder."

"Say what now?" Fury's voice ripped across the connection.

"Would you stop listening to us?"

"What plague?"

"Dion had a needle to Lillian's neck when I took him out. We recovered it."

"For fuck's sake, that would have been good to know." He could almost see Fury throwing his hands up in the air. "Do not get on that transport with that material."

"You want me to leave it here?" Billy asked, and

Lillian stopped and turned to look at him questioningly.

"No. Damn it." Fury's curse-laden rant went on.

Asp turned to look at him. "You have what on your person?"

Lillian lifted her fingers to her lips and nodded toward the medics who were shoving their kits into the back of the blacked-out van they'd arrived in this morning.

Asp shoved his ball cap back on his head and put his hand on his hip. "Give it to me."

"Why?"

"We're staying in Paris. Someone will come to our hotel and collect it."

"So, you will let a hotel of people be at risk but not an aircraft?" He waited for Fury's answer, but one didn't come. "Huh. I might have broken him."

Lillian blinked. "Who?"

"Fury," he replied.

She shook her head. "I don't think that's possible."

Asp motioned with his hand again. Billy pulled out the container and gave it to him. "Be careful with that."

"Thanks, I got that message in between all of

Fury's ranting." Asp held up his fist. "Whatever it takes, brother."

"As long as it takes." He bumped Asp's fist, and the assassin turned and headed to where Alex was waiting for him. Billy threw her kit in on top of everyone else's and helped her into the van before he got in the passenger side seat and looked at Specter. "Let's go home."

They pulled out after the first van holding one team, and the second van pulled in after them. All Foxtrot Team was staying in France with their team leader. They drove straight to the airport with a French police escort. After they were escorted to a massive hangar and the doors were shut, they unloaded.

"Showers have been set up at the rear of the hangar," the crew chief said from the back ramp of the bird.

"Ladies first," Billy said after everyone applauded the crew chief's announcement.

"I'll be fast," she said and headed to the partitioned area. Billy waited outside the facility until she emerged wearing a too-big uniform. Her hair was wet but combed, and she wore the same boots she'd worn and carried the padded holder for the vials she'd been given. She was putting the holder in her cargo pocket when she said, "There are ten showers, clean uniforms, and towels. You guys could have gone in."

"No." One of the docs pointed to Billy. "I don't think that was going to happen."

Billy smiled and winked at her, then held the door open for the men to head in. The medics went first. Lillian sat down beside him as he waited his turn.

"I can't believe he was there." She swung her feet because they didn't reach the ground.

"I'm glad you were there to see him. No one else would have recognized him."

She sighed and leaned into him. "When I've slept a week or two, we need to figure out what's next. Based on what I saw, Abe won't be able to work in the field for months, if ever."

"If ever?" He frowned down at her.

"Would you want to go back to work after being shot?"

Billy cocked his head. "I'm the wrong person to ask. I've done that four … no five times."

Lillian dropped her head back and looked at the ceiling of the hangar. "Definitely the wrong person to ask." She groaned and rolled her shoulders. "If he comes back to work, it could be months before he's medically cleared to be in the field. I wonder if they'll assign me a new teammate."

"So, this didn't put you off working with Guardian?" Billy watched as men started to come out of the shower area.

"No. If anything, it's made me see how much they need the Mercy Teams." She dropped her head on his shoulder. "Do you think there's a way we can work in the same geographic area? I mean, if you'd want that."

He put his arm around her shoulder. "I'm sure we can work something out. That isn't something we need to worry about now."

"It isn't?" She looked up at him.

"No. We only need to worry about getting back to my apartment and not burning the bread again."

She laughed, which was what he wanted her to do. "I'm up. I'll be back. Smelling better, I hope."

"I'll be waiting for you," she said as he stood.

He smiled and bent down for a kiss. "And I'll never take that for granted. I love you."

"I love you, too."

Billy stripped down after he selected a clean uniform and lathered up. His respect for the woman he loved elevated tenfold while working with her today. She checked in with her teams as they moved from person to person. Answered questions shouted to her by techs and docs alike.

He blinked as an idea flitted across his mind. He chuckled and dismissed it, but the thing fluttered back like an annoying ass gnat he couldn't swat away. Billy let the idea settle and thought about it as he finished his shower. Maybe … if the moon was in the right position, and he was lucky … maybe …

CHAPTER 23

Lillian stretched and reached to Billy's side of the bed. The sheets on his side were cold. She lifted her head and blinked, looking for him. A note sitting beside the clock on the bedstand caught her attention.

Had a meeting with Mike. Be back soon.
Love, B.
P.S. Go back to sleep.

She rolled over and stretched again. She wasn't going back to sleep. She would go upstairs and see Abe. He'd been brought in yesterday, and they'd visited for a short time before he practically fell asleep.

She got ready quickly, left a note for Billy, and went upstairs. She knocked on the door when she saw Adam Cassidy in the room with Abe. "Am I interrupting?"

"No, not at all. We're just going over the game plan for his little rehab stint here. We'll have him ready to go home in about a week or so."

"Thanks, Doc." Abe extended his hand to Adam.

"No problem. Do what the physical and occupational therapists say, and you'll be home to that bride of yours before you know it." Adam squeezed her shoulder on the way out.

"How are you feeling?" she asked as she walked in and lifted the computer at the foot of his bed. She read the note and then looked over at Abe.

"You tell me?" He laughed but guarded his abdomen when he did.

"Your record says you're doing very well." She shut the lid and pulled up a chair so she could sit beside him. "How's Heather?"

Abe sighed and rubbed his face with his hand. "Not happy. Cash called her after the surgery, and she flew to Paris. She made one hell of a scene at the hospital because she found out I'd been shot."

He shook his head and turned to look at her. "Lil, I'm probably not going to come back to work for Guardian. I have to take care of her and need to be there with her, not traveling across the world."

Lillian blinked and then gave a half-smile. "I figured." Her gut dropped, and the fear she'd been trying to hold back clenched her tight in its hold. "What am I going to do without you?"

Abe extended his hand, and she took it. Their skin was different, hers pale and his dark, but he was the brother she'd never had. She loved Abe as a friend, and ever since Heather had burst into his life, she knew one day, she'd lose him. Seemed she was right.

"You've got your man to take care of you. We both have someone now. It's time to go our separate ways." A tear glistened in Abe's eye. "And don't you dare go getting in any trouble. You know I'll come back and straighten your shit out. Then Heather would get mad again."

She gave a sad laugh and swatted at tears that fell over her lashes. "If you love her as much as I love Billy, I'm pretty sure we'll both be okay."

"We will be, Lil. I'm sure of it." He wiped at a tear that fell. "Cash will be here soon. I don't want him to catch me blubbering."

"Then I'm going to head out. Goodbye, Abe." She stood and wiped at her tears again.

"Goodbye, Lil," Abe said as she backed out of the room.

Lillian made her way back downstairs. She went to her apartment and got in the shower. She'd lost her best friend today. As much as she'd like to think they could stay in contact, Abe wanted his relationship with Heather, and Heather wanted him to have nothing to do with her. She wouldn't ask Abe to sneak around to talk with her, and she probably wouldn't go back up to see him. They'd said their goodbyes, hadn't they?

She was a prune by the time she got out of the shower, but she needed the time to reorder things in her mind. She would mourn the loss of their friendship, but that was part of life, wasn't it? People moved in and out. Some stayed forever, and some only for a short time. Lillian wrapped a towel around her and walked out to her bedroom.

"You okay?" Billy asked her from her bed where he was lying.

She walked over to him, dropped the towel, and slid under the covers, ending up next to him. "No. Not really. Abe won't come back to work for Guardian. We said our goodbyes."

He pulled her into him, wrapping her in his arms. The warmth of his body and the covers swaddling her seeped through the internal coldness the goodbyes had introduced. "I'm sorry. I know that hurts, babe. I wish I could change it for you."

She nodded. There was nothing else that needed to be said. He knew about her fears. They'd talked for the last month about Abe and Heather. Lillian continued to help Adam out a couple days a week and worked out every morning with Billy, but the fate of Mercy Team Five was always up to Abe. Now, she needed to start looking for a new partner. Or perhaps Guardian would just tell her with whom she'd be working.

"Do you want some good news?"

She peeked up at him from under the covers. "If you have any, now would be the time to let me have it."

"Well, I had an idea."

"No," she deadpanned.

Billy laughed. "It happens occasionally. If Abe wouldn't return, you needed a new partner or maybe a new mission, right?"

She used her fingers to pull down the blankets a bit farther. "Mission?"

He released her and moved to his side, propping his head up on his hand. "So, what do you think about the idea of deploying with me when I do overwatch duties?"

"Why?"

"We'd work as a team. I'd be there for team overwatch because most of the scenarios where one of us is called in to work with a team means there's an increased threat. I'd teach you how to be helpful to me, you know, with spotter duties, and you can train me to be helpful as a tech if needed."

Lillian propped herself up on her elbow. "That's . . ."

"Not something you're interested in?" Billy supplied.

"No, that's a good idea. But what about during downtime? You told me you didn't deploy often."

"You work here with Adam, teach any classes Guardian needs to be taught, and we, you know, get married."

Lillian huffed out a laugh. "Was that a proposal?"

"Well, no, but it could be." Billy flopped onto his back. "Man, I'm slaughtering this shit."

Lillian laughed harder. "My proposal is shit?"

Billy sprung back up. "No, no, no." He sighed heavily. "Lillian Montrose, will you marry me?"

She shook her head, then let her smile spread across her face. "Of course, I'll marry you."

Billy's hand went over his heart. "You shook your head no before you said yes. I'm having a heart attack. Save me!"

Lillian unwound herself from under the covers and moved over him. She dropped her head to his chest. "Sounds like it's ticking to me."

"Are you sure?" Billy lifted his head. "Maybe you should check lower."

Lillian laughed. "Lower?"

Billy nodded, trying to keep an innocent face. "You've never heard the expression my heart dropped?"

"No, and I don't think that's physically possible."

"It is. You should check."

She smiled and reached for his belt. "Perhaps I should." She unfastened his belt and jeans and pulled his cock out. Wrapping her hand around it she looked up at him. "I have a strong pulse."

He propped himself up on his elbows. "Are you positive?"

"I am." She nodded and gasped as he lifted and

pushed her onto her back. He framed her head with his forearms and stared down at her, smiling. "You're going to be my wife."

She nodded. "I am."

He entered her, still wearing his clothes. "Mine," he said as he found a sharp rhythm. She wrapped her legs around his back and braced herself against him. The emotions were so strong. His need for her was even stronger. She shivered and gasped as she came without the usual slow build. Her body reacting to his possessiveness, she clung to him. When he finished, he dropped to his elbows. "My wife." He kissed her collarbone. "Mine."

"Yours," she said as she ran her fingers through his hair. "Always."

He dropped to his side and pulled her against him. She continued to run her fingers through his hair and drifted through their conversation. Stopping her fingers, she asked, "Is that what you had your meeting with Mike about today?"

He opened his eyes and asked, "Sex?"

She thumped him with a finger. "No, working together."

"Oh. Yes." Billy chuckled. "Sorry, my brain is stuck on one track sometimes."

"You? Never." She laughed and cuddled closer. "He said it was okay?"

"The powers that be like the idea of you here to back up Adam. Although they sometimes have the doc from Hollister come out when Adam is gone, they like the idea of a permanent backup. The doctor from Hollister can come out if we're deployed and Adam is gone. As far as you deploying with me, they're leaving it up to you. If you want to take on that responsibility, they're willing to allow the exception."

She sighed. "I want to learn, and I can teach you. I'm not sure I want to deploy. Do I have to decide now?"

"Nope. As I said, they're happy just having you here full-time. The only thing you have to decide now is when we're tying the knot."

"Hmmm ..." She lifted and laid on his chest, looking down at him. "How fast can you get a license in South Dakota?"

"I don't know. I'm betting pretty fast." He gave her that sexy half-smile.

"Then you should probably work on that."

"That's not a date."

"Yes, it is. I'll marry you as soon as you have the license."

Lillian flipped onto her back, and Billy jumped out of the bed and ran out of the room.

"Billy!" she yelled after him.

He zoomed back into the room. "What?"

"Fasten your pants!" She pointed at his jeans.

"Right." He shoved himself back in and zipped up. "I'll be back. I love you."

"I love you, too!" she yelled and heard her apartment door shut with a slam. She closed her eyes and smiled. Life was full of twists and turns. You never knew where it would take you, but she thanked God for the plane trip to South Dakota. It took her to the snarky, sexy, funny man who was perfect for her.

EPILOGUE

Jason King sat across from Gabriel and Frank Marshall. He leaned forward and pointed to the name on the list that had been on his scope since Dr. Christopher Whitehead had died. "Anne Truman, the Undersecretary of State, Security Division. She was promoted from her position within the Department of Defense by our current POTUS."

Gabriel sighed. "She would be the likely appointee, true."

Frank Marshall took a sip of his coffee. "She's the one you suspect was involved in the release of information during the Whitehead issue?"

Jason nodded. "She was the only one who was told what was going on."

"But we can't prove she released any information," Frank said.

"Correct," Jason replied.

Gabriel ran his finger around the rim of his coffee cup. "And how is she involved with Abrasha Molchalin?"

"In the vaguest sense," Jason admitted. "She went to a semester of college overseas. Molchalin's daughter was in three of her four classes that semester."

"And that's the only tie-in you have?" Gabriel asked.

"It is, but I know it was her. Who else had the Secretary of State's ear? The mission in France could have been unrecoverable for Guardian."

"But you and your people didn't let that happen," Frank reminded him.

"It came close." Jason sighed. "She's involved. Molchalin's the money."

"The raid on his business found nothing," Frank said quietly.

"And yet they had all the equipment to process what we have in that sample," Gabriel said and sat forward. "We can monitor her, but we'll need more solid information before we can take it to POTUS."

"Phone? Home? Digital and video?" Jason asked.

Gabriel glanced at Frank. The old cowboy shrugged. "Figure it's best to keep tabs on a person who's under a threat, right?"

"What?" Jason frowned.

"Well, now, son, I heard you had some credible information that someone has it in for this woman. Someone thinks maybe she's going to be a target."

"You mean besides me?" Jason laughed.

"No," Frank said the single word. "We're protecting our country's finest. If anyone finds out, you have files. Lots of files showing how you're protecting her. Dated back to the time of White-head's death. A credible source. You're just doing your job. POTUS can't argue with that."

"And this is one of the reasons I wouldn't let you leave this company." Gabriel chuckled.

"Now, I believe we have a reception to go to. Billy and Lillian got hitched last week. Lyric done cooked up enough food for the entire state."

"Or Asp," Gabriel said as he stood.

"I'll be there in a minute. Elliot wanted to talk with me. Would you send him in?"

"Done. Make sure you get over there. Your mom wants to fuss over you a bit, and you'll let her."

"Yes, sir." Jason smiled at his stepfather.

Elliot knocked on the door to the underground office Jason used when he was in South Dakota. "Do you have a moment, sir?"

"I do. What's up?" Jason leaned back and looked up at the team leader who had taken care of his family since he and Faith had married.

"Sir, I think it's time for a change." Elliot swallowed hard. "I need a change. I'd like to lateral into personal security. Monte is a good man, and he's damn smart. He'd be a good replacement for me."

Jason drew a deep breath. "How long have you been thinking about this?"

"Since the Siege, sir. I … I was supposed to be on duty. If I had been …"

"And you've worked with Dr. Wheeler?"

"I have. I've got the green light for the lateral."

Jason stood up. "Elliot, I don't want to lose you. I trust you more than anyone else, but I won't hold you in a position eating you from the inside."

Elliot nodded. "Thank you, sir."

"Get with Sonya and start the paperwork."

Jason used his cane and walked over to his friend. He extended his hand. "Thank you for everything you've done for Faith, the kids, and me. If you ever want to come home, there will be a place for you with us. Always."

"Thank you, sir." Elliot nodded and shook his hand. "It has been an honor."

Jason watched the man walk out the door and then scrubbed his face with his hand. No matter how much he wanted the man to stay with them, he had to let him go. His gut had warned him that something was in the works with Elliot for quite a while now.

He sighed and looked back at the charred map behind his desk. The job they did could consume a person, no matter the position. He prayed Elliot could outrun his ghosts. Many hadn't. But for the rest of them … Well, they'd do whatever it took for as long as it took. The world was filled with dangerous people, but as long as there was a breath left in him, there would be Guardians ready to protect and serve.

. . .

Elliot survived the Siege, but will he be able to survive his next assignment? Click here to read that story.

Did you miss Billy's backstory? You can read how he and Asp met again in Asp's book.

ALSO BY KRIS MICHAELS

Kings of the Guardian Series

Jacob: Kings of the Guardian Book 1

Joseph: Kings of the Guardian Book 2

Adam: Kings of the Guardian Book 3

Jason: Kings of the Guardian Book 4

Jared: Kings of the Guardian Book 5

Jasmine: Kings of the Guardian Book 6

Chief: The Kings of Guardian Book 7

Jewell: Kings of the Guardian Book 8

Jade: Kings of the Guardian Book 9

Justin: Kings of the Guardian Book 10

Christmas with the Kings

Drake: Kings of the Guardian Book 11

Dixon: Kings of the Guardian Book 12

Passages: The Kings of Guardian Book 13

Promises: The Kings of Guardian Book 14

The Siege: Book One, The Kings of Guardian Book 15

The Siege: Book Two, The Kings of Guardian Book 16

A Backwater Blessing: A Kings of Guardian Crossover Novella

Montana Guardian: A Kings of Guardian Novella

Guardian Defenders Series

Gabriel

Maliki

John

Jeremiah

Frank

Creed

Sage

Bear

Billy

Elliot

Guardian Security Shadow World

Anubis (Guardian Shadow World Book 1)

Asp (Guardian Shadow World Book 2)

Lycos (Guardian Shadow World Book 3)

Thanatos (Guardian Shadow World Book 4)

Tempest (Guardian Shadow World Book 5)

Smoke (Guardian Shadow World Book 6)

Reaper (Guardian Shadow World Book 7)

Phoenix (Guardian Shadow World Book 8)

Valkyrie (Guardian Shadow World Book 9)

Flack (Guardian Shadow World Book 10)

Ice (Guardian Shadow World Book 11)

Malice (Guardian Shadow World Book 12)

Harbinger (Guardian Shadow World Book 13)

Centurion (Guardian Shadow World Book 14)

Hollister (A Guardian Crossover Series)

Andrew (Hollister-Book 1)

Zeke (Hollister-Book 2)

Declan (Hollister- Book 3)

Ken (Hollister - Book 4)

Barry (Hollister - Book 5)

Hope City

Hope City - Brock

HOPE CITY - Brody- Book 3

Hope City - Ryker - Book 5

Hope City - Killian - Book 8

Hope City - Blayze - Book 10

The Long Road Home

Season One:

My Heart's Home

Season Two:

Searching for Home (A Hollister-Guardian Crossover Novel)

Season Three:

A Home for Love (A Hollister Crossover Novel)

STAND-ALONE NOVELS

A Heart's Desire - Stand Alone

Hot SEAL, Single Malt (SEALs in Paradise)

Hot SEAL, Savannah Nights (SEALs in Paradise)

Hot SEAL, Silent Knight (SEALs in Paradise)

Join my newsletter for fun updates and release information!

>>>Kris' Newsletter<<<

ABOUT THE AUTHOR

Wall Street Journal and USA Today Bestselling Author, Kris Michaels is the alter ego of a happily married wife and mother. She writes romance, usually with characters from military and law enforcement backgrounds.

Made in United States

Made in United States
Troutdale, OR
03/02/2024